James Whelan

Catena Aurea

Or, a golden chain of evidences

James Whelan

Catena Aurea
Or, a golden chain of evidences

ISBN/EAN: 9783337045326

Printed in Europe, USA, Canada, Australia, Japan

Cover: Foto ©Andreas Hilbeck / pixelio.de

More available books at **www.hansebooks.com**

CATENA AUREA,

OR

A GOLDEN CHAIN OF EVIDENCES

DEMONSTRATING FROM

"ANALYTICAL TREATMENT OF HISTORY,"

THAT

PAPAL INFALLIBILITY IS NO NOVELTY.

————·——

A MEMORIAL OF THE PAPAL JUBILEE,

JUNE 16, 1871,

TO HONOR THE "ANNOS PETRI COMPLETOS" OF OUR HOLY FATHER,

POPE PIUS THE GREAT.

————··————

BY AN OLD CATHOLIC.

_____ '' \'· ⊂|∩⊓

" While others contribute their gold and their silver to the service
of the tabernacle, why should not I contribute my humble offerings,
at least of hair-cloth and skins?"—St. Jerome, *Preface to Vulgate.*

————·——·——

ST. JOSEPH'S COLLEGE, PERRY COUNTY, OHIO.
1871.

Remarks to the Courteous Reader.

1. This little book has been prepared, principally, for a plain and honest minded class of Catholic and non-Catholic readers in the towns and country places of Perry and contiguous counties, within the missionary limits served from St. Joseph's College. There are no pretensions to elegance of style or profundity of learned research. Facts of history—true facts which the reader CAN recognize and MUST accept as true facts of history—constitute our subject matter.

2. A cherished desire, wise or unwise, on the part of the author, to foster and patronize "home industry," induced him to commit his manuscript to the tender mercies of a small JOB OFFICE in a not very large but thrifty city. The mechanical process of "getting out" the pamphlet has been slow and tedious—the process has been "going on" ever since June sixteenth, when "copy" was delivered to the printer with an understanding that "copies" were to be in the hands of readers in a week, or in two weeks at furthest. The number of pages, however, exceed the original calculation. In fact, the author, at first, intended the manuscript to "come out" a LITTLE PAMPHLET of a few sections, and the reader will notice that, frequently, in these pages, he uses that designation, but it seems that "waiting for proof" has had the effect of emboldening the LITTLE PAMPHLET to "put in an appearance" manifesting all the airs of a SMALL BOOK !

3. On page 8, we give the number of Popes, including both St. Peter and Pius IX, as being two hundred and fifty-three; we should have written two hundred and fifty-four. Pius IX is the two hundred and fifty-fourth Bishop of Rome, including St Peter. Stephen II was elected March 27, A. D. 752, and died within three days, without being inaugurated. He was a true Pope, but is passed over in most of the lists. In like manner, and for some like reason, certain writers pass over the names of one or two other short-lived Popes who shone only for a passing moment upon the Pontifical throne. The learned Archbishop Kenrick, "PRIMACY, and THEOL. DOGMAT.," gives the list of Popes as containing 251 names. Darras enumerates all who have been true Popes, and the number, AFTER St. Peter, is given as 253—including St. Peter, 254.

4. Page 10 insinuates the number of professing Catholics in the whole world—spiritual subjects of Pius IX—as being in round numbers three hundred millions. Published statistics of the population of the entire world are very uncertain data whereby to compute the aggregate number of adherents to the faith of the Holy Catholic Church. From data which to himself appear to be satisfactory the writer is inclined to the opinion that, in round numbers, his estimate of three hundred millions is a nearer approximation to the true figures than is the time-honored GUESS of two hundred. A determinate number, however, cannot be given as one of our proved facts. On that point the author assumes his position to be nothing more than a most probable one.

5. The Catena Aurea has not been compiled for the learned, nor for those who have access to heavier and more costly works. The view of the writer has been, solely, to impart certain informing ideas upon an interesting and important topic of the day to an unpretending class of general readers whom the very sight of "a big and dear book" would affright, but who seldom fail of courage to purchase and "go through" a nice looking pamphlet which has a good many resting places—provided the pamphlet be cheap and the print not "too hard on the eyes." For that class of readers for whom it has been prepared, the author has aimed to make the production a readable little book. If he has succeeded, it is well,—if not, his intention at least was good.

6. The author would say to all the members of the Goody Critic family that he is supremely indifferent to their silly fault-finding comments. These pages do not claim to be a FINISHED piece of literary composition. Far otherwise. Our chapters will fulfill the designed end of their creation, and will be, at least of SOME use in the world, which, generally, is not the case with that class of carping humanity ycleped poking, fault-seeking critics. The writer would say to dear Goody and Co. that the principle upon which this production has been constructed is "HUC UNDIQUE GAZÆ" The honey of truth has been sucked from a variety of flowers in the "Eden of Literature." The author will be his own reviewing critic, and make to his generous readers a candid avowal that, in this "Golden Chain of Evidences" whatsoever is really good is not new, and whatsoever is new is not likely to be found very good.

7. For the rest, if there be aught in these pages—a paragraph—a sentence—a word—a chance punctuation mark—that can possibly be tortured into the semblance of a meaning which our Infallible Pio Nono would disapprove, the unworthy author, here and now, at once and forever, reprobates that meaning.

No book, not even the Holy Bible, it is said, was ever printed without *some* "errors of the types." There are a few of that kind of errors, here and there, through the pages of Catena Aurea. A printed word, now and then, exhibits evidence of a type misplaced, a type redundant, or a type deficient—but no error of greater moment in any way affecting the sense of a word or sentence. It is needless, therefore, to specify misprints more particularly. Unimportant as the said paucity of misprints may be, the author hereby appologizes for them, and offers as his only excuse that they were "accomplished facts" before the signatures containing them came finally under his own eyes. Whatever may have been with regard to delay of publication, the separate papers of this edition were rather hurriedly prepared by the author. In a future "remodeled, enlarged, amended and corrected edition" it is to be hoped that no misprints will be overlooked.

St. Joseph's, Perry County, Ohio,
    Festival of St. Rose de Lima, August 30, 1871.

TABLE OF CONTENTS.

PAGE.

Our Inscription......... 5
Our Mite Offering.. 7
I. Introductory......... 11
II. Some Fiction about a New Departure.................. 12
III. Some Facts about a New Departure...... 13
IV. The Situation Past and Present........................ 17
V. The New Departure Rises to Explain........ 21
VI. Defining an Article of Faith and Making One......... 27
VII. The Term Infallibility Defined............................ 29
VIII. A Mischievous Logomachy Settled........................ 32
IX. The Solid Foundation of our Faith........................ 37
X. Reason Demonstrates the Catholic Church............... 39
XI. Practical Application of our First Principle............. 41
XII. Exodus of the Jewish—Advent of the Catholic Church. 46
XIII. Christ Organizes the Holy Catholic Church.............. 49
XIV. The Catholic Church a Visible Fact in the World.... 53
XV. St. Paul's Official Visit to St. Peter..................... 57
XVI. St. Peter Founds the Roman Church..................... 61
XVI. Council of Jerusalem.... 62
XVII. St. Paul's Testimony about the Roman Church......... 65
XVIII. The Fourth Bishop of Rome, St. Clement............. 67
XIX. Our Historical Positions are Impregnable.............. 69
XX. Roman Supremacy a Public Fact from earliest days 80
XXI. A Retrospect of the Situation............................ 88
XXII. Conciliar Evidences—First Ecumenical Council....... 95
XXIII. Sec. Ecum. Coun.—Can. of Holy Scriptures Defined 100
XXIV. Third Ecumenical Council at Ephesus. 105
XXV. Fourth Ecumenical Council at Chalcedon...............106
XXVI. Pope Hormisdas and the Orientals.......................109
XXVII. Sixth Ecumenical Council............................ 111
XXVIII. Eighth Ecumenical Council........ 113
XXIX. Ecumenical Council at Lyons.............................115
XXX. Ecumenical Council at Constance........................117
XXXI. Ecumenical Council at Florence...........................123
XXXI. Ecumenical Councils of Lateran and Trent............126
XXXII. ECUMENICAL COUNCIL OF THE VATICAN..............128
XXXIII. Protestantism, 1530, recognized Papal Infallibility.....135
XXXIV. Crumbs of Comfort for anti-Catholic Prophets.........150
XXXV. How to Seek and Find Catholic Truth................157
XXXVI. A Concluding Illustration................................159

APPROBATION OF THE ORDINARY.

We have read with much interest the advance sheets of the CATENA AUREA, and cordially approve its publication.

SYLVESTER H. ROSECRANS,
Bishop of Columbus.

August 19, 1871.

OUR INSCRIPTION.

Considering the object, and the subject, of this production, the writer thinks that it cannot be more appropriately "home-inscribed," than to the dear Catholic people of Perry county,--the cradle-county of Catholicity in Ohio. A vast number of that faithful population are the lineal descendants, all of them are the representative successors, of the " Primitive Christians" of this great Commonwealth. In a particular manner, an expression of grateful remembrance is due to the few surviving old folk, and, to the octogenarian surviving Patriarch, the first known Resident Priest, and Catholic Pastor, within the boundary limits of this vast State called Ohio, from the reapers of the Catholic blessings whereof they were the sowers who sowed the good seed. The pastor and the flock, who, A. D. 1818, formed the first, and, for some time, the only Catholic congregation that could worship God within the walls of a dedicated temple, must not be forgotten.

The present, and the future generations of Catholics around the dear old Catholic centre-spot, the fondly remembered "Old St. Joseph's," ought not to forget the faithful people, nor forget the zealous and self-sacrising Pastors of the olden time. They are deserving of pious remembrance, the good Catholic Priests, and the faithful Catholic laity, who used to meet, Sundays and Holy-days, at "the little log church," which, in those days was--the great church--the great Catholic centre of a parochial circle, whereof, Cleveland and Wheeling, Toledo and Cincinnati, were far within the periphery.

Embalmed in holiest recollections of the Faithful are, and ever shall be, the names of the zealous Fathers, Edward Dominic Fenwick, Augustine Hill, Richard Pius Miles, Joseph O'Leary, Thomas Martin, James Hyacinth Clarkson, Augustine P. Anderson, Charles P. Montgomery, Anthony O'Brien, Eugene H. Pozzo, Charles D. Boling, Philip D. Noon, and others, whom our good Lord hath taken unto himself. The writer will be excused for not putting upon paper, just now, any mere verbal expression of the cherished sentiments of pious and grateful memory toward the two surviving servants of God,--Very Rev Joseph T. Jarboe, and the Patriarchal octogenarian, Nicholas Dominic Young.

Thoughts of the Rt. Rev., Very Rev., and Rev. Fathers whose names are in holy memory at "old St. Joseph's," and in the neighboring Congregations, suggest the revered names of Holy Religion's first noble benefactors, in these parts. They are not likely to pass into unnoticed obscurity. So long as the magnificent churches of our vicinity called "St. Joseph's," "Holy Trinity," "St. Thomas Aquinas," "St. Patricks," shall occupy the ground upon which they are located, so long cannot be forgotten these names--Jacob Dittoe, Senior, and Catharine his wife; John Finck, Senior, and Mary his wife; John S. Duggan, and Barbara his wife; Alexander Clark, and Mary his wife; the original donors of grounds for church purposes;--besides other benefactors whose years date not back to so early a period in our history. To the dead and the living God's mercy. Amen.

OUR MITE-OFFERING.

THIS MEMORIAL BROCHURE is commenced in the name of the Father, and of the Son, and of the Holy Ghost. It is to be regarded as an humble mite-offering, expressive of the fond attachment, and devotedness, of the writer, and, of the faithful Catholic people whose earliest recollections cluster around "Old St. Joseph's," Perry county, Ohio, to the CAUSE, and—to the PERSON, of their INFALLIBLE HOLY FATHER, POPE PIUS THE GREAT.

THE MITE, in itself, possesses no material intrinsic value; but, the filial sentiments which prompt it into a tangible existence as a memorial-token, can be surpassed by none among the devoted children of Holy Faith,-- though, of their abundance, *they* may be able to make offerings of "their gold and their silver," while *we*, of our poverty, can make offerings of nothing but of "haircloth and skins," which may, however, serve to cover the outside of the tabernacle, and protect, in that humble way, the rich ornaments and treasures within. (Exodus xxxvi.) Treasures of earth we have none; but, other things which are ours to give, are freely given--are given without restricting qualification. Heartfelt sympathy--protest in the face of the world against all agents of the devil, wicked oppressors of the Holy Roman See--open confession of entire Catholic Faith as taught by our IN-FALLIBLE PIUS IX, Bishop of Rome -spiritual obedience without slightest mental reservation,--outward manifestation of devotedness to the Holy Vatican

Prisoner held in chains by the Sardinian Herod,-- readiness to hear, and to heed, the voice of our Sovereign Pontiff, in whatsoever way that voice may reach us-- these things, and such as these, are at our own disposal, and we offer them, accordingly. To the successor of St. Peter the tributes which we have named are eminently due; and, *our* Peter-pence, in that currency, shall be paid even until death.

As to time, the occasion of our mite-offering is--the celebration of a GRAND PAPAL JUBILEE, June 16, 1871. This occasion is the first Jubilee of the kind which christendom has ever celebrated. Since the Ascension of our Lord, there have been two hundred and fifty-three Bishops of Rome, Popes, including in the enumeration both ST. PETER and PIUS THE NINTH. St. Peter having been Vicar of Jesus Christ, and Supreme Head, on earth, of the Holy Catholic Church for about thirteen years, came, *then*, to Rome, in the second year of the Emperor Claudius, A. D. 42. At Rome, St. Peter permanently *fixed* his Apostolic *Cathedram*, and, as Bishop of Rome, St. Peter governed the Universal Church of Christ on earth *"viginti quinque annos completos,"*...*twenty-five years completed*. Since the going to heaven of St. Peter, A. D. 67, two hundred and fifty-one Popes have lived, and died. No one among them all ever "saw," in the Roman Pontificate, the "annos completos,"...the the completed years of Rome's first Bishop. Our Holy Father PIUS THE NINTH, June 16, 1871, *completes* the "years of Peter." Hence the Grand Papal Jubilee, on the above named date. The ecclesiastical day of the Catholic Church, for purposes of her liturgical services, commences with what is called *first vespers*. The *liturgical* anniversary of the election of *Pio Nono*, very properly, is registered for commemoration in the Holy Mass, and in other Divine Services, on June 17, because the Holy Father was elected *late* in the day, after all the Divine Services proper for that *civil* day were ended...he was elected some hours after the liturgical services of June 17th had commenced. The liturgical anniversary, or. the *ecclesiastical* day, June 17th, begins when the sun is hastening in its decline, on the civil June 16th. This *memorial-brochure*, therefore, bears the proper *civil* date, June 16, 1871.

Our Holy Father having seen the "years of Peter," may it please God that he live yet, "*ad multos annos.*" Grant it our God! that Pius the Ninth may live to see the speedy execution of what Thou hast sworn against "the gentiles who are raging; and the people who are devising vain things; and the kings of the earth who are standing up; and the princes who are met together against the Lord and against his Christ." (Psalm ii.) May Pius the Ninth live to see Thee "Do to them as Thou doest to Madian, and to Sisera, and to all the princes who say: Let us possess the Sanctuary of God for an inheritance. O our God! let them know that the Lord is Thy name, and that Thou alone art the most High over all the earth." *Psalm* lxxxii, *King James'* lxxxiii Holy Vicar of Christ now in chains for Christ's sake, we, thy distant American children, taught of Holy Dominic's white-robed " Order of Truth "--so styled from the Roman See itself,--we, thy American children taught of the "Sacred Order of Preachers" in our "St. Joseph's Province, United States of North America," salute thee, and kiss thy chains! Soon will it be that "He who dwelleth in heaven shall laugh at thy enemies, and the Lord shall deride them, He shall speak to them in His anger, and trouble them in His rage." *Psalm* ii. Soon shall thy enemies have cause to know and confess that thou are the annointed King,--

God-appointed, to rule over Sion his holy mountain, and to preach his commandment, well knowing in whom to place thy trust." Thou art filled with certainty as to knowledge of results speedily to follow present afflictions. Thou kneelest beside the tomb of Peter, to protest against, and to pray for, thy persecutors. Thou dost invite thy obedient children of faith to unite with Thee in protest, and in prayer, and in good works, that the end may soon be, and that the avenging hand of Thy God may be staid from further protracted chastisement of vengeance upon all wicked plotters "against the Lord and against His Christ." "Come, my children, come, let us unite in prayer," is the invitation that has sounded forth from beside St. Peter's tomb. The invitation has been heard. From pole to pole, from first meridian around to first meridian again, there has been harmonious unison of acclamation, causing thy enemies to quake. Significant tones of thunder have resounded to them from Thy devoted ones, and the sound was not meaningless.

"Come, my children come--let us unite in prayer," was the fatherly request.

"We are coming, Holy Father, coming--we are coming, three hundred millions strong," was the acclamatory, dutiful response.

Catholics! than our present Sovereign Pontiff, no greater Bishop of Rome ever governed the Universal Church since the days of St. Peter--no greater Prince ever ruled over a people. Why shall not we begin, even now, to name him--PIUS THE GREAT!

PAPAL INFALLIBILITY NO NOVELTY.

CHAPTER FIRST.

I.

INTRODUCTORY.

In these days, the subject of Infallibility deserves some study, and a good deal of thought. It is a frequent theme of conversation in the social circle; newspaperdom treats *at* the topic, with a plenitude of ignorance. Non-Catholics ought to know something that *is* true about a matter concerning which, they hear much and tell more. Catholics ought to be ready and prompt, when the question is sprung, to pop a clinching answer at all enquiring truth-seekers. In this country, a vast number of persons outside the pale of the Catholic Church, seek, and receive, *all* their knowledge of things, sacred and profane, from "the papers," or from "the pulpit," or from "the stump." Considering the sources whence, alone, the "Average Protestant" takes all of his, *said to be*, positive knowledge of religion and history, it is no wonder that, when Catholic matters come upon the carpet, the very best looking average Protestant, invariably, makes a mean and nasty show of himself to the sight, and in the hearing, of sensible people who *do* know

something. The poor *"average,"* who makes essays against
Pope or Popery, taking his cue from "the papers," or,
from "the pulpit," or from "the stump," must be, always,
sadly uninformed, or terribly misinformed. If neither
uninformed nor misinformed...and if, yet, he takes the
cue, and sticks to it...then, he is an arrant knave! In
nearly every circle of social life one may meet with a
representative specimen of this cue-taking class. Dear
"Average,!" an *"Old Catholic"* begs that you take this
little pamphlet, make it your *text-book*, master its contents, so as to have all its points at your tongue's end,...
then, *talk away*, without dread or danger of making a
fool of yourself.

II.

SOME FICTION ABOUT A "NEW DEPARTURE."

We have news from Europe that certain individuals,
of the little kingdom of Bavaria, have revolted against
the authority of the Catholic church; but more particularly, against *a new* article of faith, which the Ecumenical Council of the Vatican, Fourth Session, July 18,
1870, *defined* and *decreed*, with all Conciliar and Papal
solemnization, and authority. We are told that *the* few,
of Bavaria, intend to "start" a National Church, with
Cæsar as supreme head. Cæsar is to be *their* Pope.
Our gentlemanly friend who is known to us under the
familar name *"Average,"* retails information from "the
papers," that the most learned man in all Germany
gave up the Catholic Church, and said good-bye, forever,
to the Pope, because that learned man would not give
his full assent to the *new* article which, the Pope, and
the Bishops, tried to force upon his better judgment.

The platform of the "new departure" in Bavaria, was constructed by the distinguished theologian and historian, Herr Ignatz Von Dœllinger, assisted, and · encouraged, principally, by Dr. Michelis, Dr. Shulte, Dr. Friederich, and Professor Huber. Dr. Dœllinger is the responsible head and front of the whole movement. The Doctor puts forward as the chief, indeed, as the only, reason, which caused,...nay, forced,...*him* to secede, *was*, "deep study of historical facts." It is alleged that "*Analytical treatment of history*" most emphatically *demonstrates* plain facts "in contradiction with" the new made article of faith; and that, therefore, the Council, and its Supreme Head, the Pope, have defined a thing to be an article of Divine Faith, which thing, is provable from history to be a glaring error, absolutely "in contradiction with" *demonstrated* facts. There seems to be no mumbling of the question in that statement. The case has been fairly entered, and the grounds have been clearly enunciated.

The Bavarian "new departure" promises to build a secession church, make Cæsar its pope, and supercede the Holy Ghost's influence in *their* branch of the Christian Church, by something which they choose to call "*Analytical treatment of history*"...a stuffed "Guy!" Now, fools may run after, or with, the "Guy;" that is no fault of TRUE HISTORY; it argues only a misfortune of the deluded fools.

III.

SOME FACTS ABOUT THAT "NEW DEPARTURE."

Doctor Von Dœllinger, an aged Catholic Priest, and a widely celebrated Professor of Theology and of History, in the University of Munich, Bavaria, a devoted courtier,

and, withal, a proud man, refuses to hear the church.
(St. Matthew xviii. 17.) Holy Church, in her wisdom,
has judged it advisable, at this time, to *"define* anew"
with regard to one particular point of the ancient
Faith, namely:--the "Inerrancy of the Supreme Head of
the Church" when, officially, he declares what is true
Catholic Faith. Our Doctor always professed to "believe
without doubting," professes, now, to "believe without
doubting," that the Catholic Church in communion with
the Bishop of Rome is, always has been, and always
must be, absolutely Infallible, when teaching Faith and
Morals. The Pope and the Bishops, under omnipotent
influence of the Holy Ghost, cannot teach error. Here
are a few propositions which the Doctor, we presume,
never doubted;--no one could be a true Catholic and
doubt them:--

1. A general Council must be assembled by, or with
the consent, of the Bishop of Rome; or its proceedings
are all null and void.

2. Whatsoever a General Council may decree about
Faith and Morals, when the decree has been solemnly
confirmed by the Bishop of Rome, the authority of that
decree must be considered infallible.

3. Suppose an impossible case. A large *majority* of the
Bishops of a General Council, lawfully assembled, draws
up, and signs, a decree about Faith and Morals; a small
minority of the Council does not concur with the greater
number; the minority draws up, and signs *another* decree
at variance with the decree of the majority; both decrees
are presented to the Pope for confirmation; the larger
number may be imagined as being *five hundred*, and the
smaller number as *fifty*, or less; the Pope examines, and,

without giving reasons, he solemnly confirms the decree of the *fifty*. What then? The five hundred must accept the decree of "the fifty" as an infallible authority, equally as if, unanimously, the five hundred and fifty AND THE POPE, had concurred from the beginning! What gives to the presented decree of "the fifty" the absolute character of infallibility? Not their own signatures, for there are *ten fifties* "in contradiction with" one *fifty*. But what gives the infallibility? Not the acceptance of "the five hundred," for they do not accept until the Bishop of Rome affixes a solemn confirmation, and proclaims what is the true faith. But what gives the infallible authority? The five hundred go over to the opinion of the fifty; the majority is then with the Pope; the Pope *has* decreed; the great body of Bishops accepts; the authority of the decree is infallible; binding the whole world—was that it? But, "the five hundred went over," precisely because, and for no other reason than, that the decree was infallible before one of them started to "go over." If any one refused to "go over," after the decree had been proclaimed, that one, by the very act of refusing to "go over," would proclaim himself, in the face of the christian world, an impugner of the known truth, and a heretic; outside the pale of the One, Holy, Catholic, church of Jesus Christ. That was the reason they "went over," and not to impart infallibility to a Papal decree.

The case is an assumed one, which never has had a practical illustration in the life of the church. It is referred to, here, as an apt illustration, descriptive of what the universal rule of the church has been, always, as to the point intended to be illustrated. There has been a great deal of metaphysical hair-splitting, and a vast amount of subtile--subtle is the more proper word--

theorizing, in a manner, and for purposes which we will not undertake to explain just now. Our object is to come at the plain point of Papal Infallibility, as defined by decree, July 18, 1870, and, to put that plain point into such words that the reader may find no difficulty in comprehending them. The point seems to us to be very plainly put forward in the assumed case, and the rule of faith of the church is not an obscure matter that needs much defining. Men have theorized in the dark, or obscurely in day light, but no man, bishop, or priest, or layman, did ever remain within the one fold of Jesus Christ, as a recognized child of the Catholic Church, who, in any practical manner, directly or indirectly, denied, or refused to obey, as in the assumed case, where "the five hundred" did not carry Infallibility with them when they "went over," but, recognized it after they arrived at the end of the trip. There they found Peter, and asked him. Peter defined for them! gave them the true faith, confirmed them as Christ had commanded him to do, and, after that, sent each one to his own see, that, from his own Episcopal chair, the returned Bishop might impart to his own flock the spiritual food of sound faith which he himself had received from the Supreme Feeder of the entire fold. In the present instance, the nucleus of the thought about "the five hundred" and "the fifty" is in one of the brain-cells of the writer, lodged there, some years ago, from the pages of no enemy of gallicanism. "Tournely" treats the subject,--and so do, also, nearly all the writers who have been set down as the most bitter Gallicans. All admit, and openly announce, the true practical faith of the Catholic Church to be, and, always, to have been, as in the given assumed case. One could not be a Catholic, at all, and not make the admission, if brought to the test.

IV.

Every reading Catholic knows that propositions first and second, on page 14, set forth the relation which the Pope holds, by divine right, toward a general council and its proceedings. Until the sixteenth century, Christendom was a unit in admitting the divinely established prerogatives of the Bishop of Rome, in manner as literally expressed in the propositions. That Jesus Christ established ONE Church, and that one an *infallible* Church, no nominal Christians worth noticing did ever deny, save, only, the "sects," commonly called Protestant. When and wherefore the original reformers, thirteen years after the birth of Protestantism, resolved upon a systematic denial of both the infallibility of the Church, and the supreme authority of the Pope, will be stated toward the end of our little book. The reformers *had* reasons for pretending to believe in opposition to all Christendom, East and West, but the reasons were not inspired from heaven, as the unbiassed reader must confess, when we bring the records to bear upon the facts in the case.

The first eight Ecumenical Councils were held in the East. The Greek schism was consummated A. D. 1053. It continues to this ay. On the sixth of July, 1274, Emperor and Prelates of the East, at the General Council of Lyons, under Pope Gregory X., abjured the schism. East and West, once more, were united in the one fold of Jesus Christ. The union was not of long duration. On the sixth of July, A. D. 1439, at the General Council of Florence, under Pope Eugenius IV., the Greek Emperor, with all his bishops save one Mark of Ephesus, sought and obtained, once more, admission into the bosom of the Holy Catholic Church. A tumultuous populace was easily stirred up in opposition to the ratified union. A few aspiring renegades harangued, and excited the multitude to clamorous outcries against submission to the spiritual authority of the Bishop of Rome. The Emperor was weak, the prelates were not strong, the perfidious Greeks had abused God's abundant graces until the measure of their iniquities was full to the brim. Again the cry became general... "We will not have this man...the Bishop of Rome...to rule over us." God heard the cry. In the fourteenth year after the last reunion of the East and West, May 29, 1453, Almighty God turned over Constantinople and the perfidious Greeks to the tender guardianship of Turkish despots.

We thought it advisable to pen a notice of the preceding facts, for the purpose of facilitating to the general reader a fuller comprehension of the past and present situation of Christendom in its relation to the ever-admitted Supreme Headship of the Bishop of Rome. Until the advent of Protestantism, and, indeed, until A. D. 1530, all Christendom of the West, from the day of its conversion, had but one voice regarding the status of the Bishop of Rome in relation to the Universal Church. Until A. D. 1053, and, indeed, so late as 1439, all Christendom of the East, represented by the bishops, Emperor and magnates, had but one voice regarding the same subject. The Eastern churches have always admitted, and still admit, the infallible authority of the Church in teaching. The Oriental churches not in communion with Rome simply deny that the supreme authority is vested in the Bishop of Rome, and assert that it is vested in the general council of bishops. Yet, to this day, the schismatic Greeks confess their inability to hold an Ecumenical Council, because it is ordained by the ancient canons that such a council can be held only under the presidency of the Patriarch of Rome. Reader, do you comprehend the situation? We think so. Further on, details will be more explicit. Infallibility of the Church being admitted, our third proposition, page 14, about "the Pope," "the fifty," and "the five hundred," shows how it is that Infallibility is not a result of a majority of votes cast by individual fallibles, but it is the result of Christ's promise to Peter and Peter's successors. *St. Luke* xxii, 32. The learned Dr. Dœllinger does not take position against the resulting conclusion from assumed illustrative case number 3, nor is he disposed to question the accuracy of statements made by the two other propositions. He is "in contradiction with" himself, to be sure, by refusing to hear the Council of the Vatican confirmed by the Pope; but what man can voluntarily maintain known falsehood without becoming, over and over again, "in woful contradiction" with himself? The good professor has no intention of analyzing history against the truth of these loud-speaking facts, to wit:

1. There has never been an instance of a Pope who proposed, to be believed by the Church, any doctrine that was contrary to the sacred rules of Faith revealed by Jesus Christ.

2. There has never been an instance where one Pope proposed something to be believed, which was in contradiction with something that had been proposed, previously, by another Pope.

3. There has never been an instance where something was proposed, to be believed as an article of Faith, which was, ever afterward, reconsidered by Council or Pope.

4. There has never been an instance where a Pope has proposed something to be believed, which was not, at once, accepted and acted upon, by the Universal Church, either assembled in council or dispersed.

5. There has never been an instance where heresies and false teachings were brought to the judicial notice of the Church, that they were not condemned by the authority of the Bishoy of Rome, alone,...and the condemnation accepted and acted upon, without further examination, by the Universal Church.

What is it, then, about which the head centre of the new departure threatens so fearfully to analyze history? Goodness knows! Let us turn to our friend and ask for an explanation.

CHAPTER SECOND

V.

THE ' NEW DEPARTURE" RISES TO EXPLAIN.

The writer begs to invite attention to four propositions which he has condensed from the "Pastoral letter" of the Archbishop of Munich, addressed to the priests and people of his diocese, and dated Easter Sunday of 1871. The Archbishop tells his priests and people that Doctor Von Dœllinger, who had deservedly held high position in the Church, had been summoned to give assent to the decrees of the Vatican council, fourth session, July 18, 1870,—and that the said Doctor Von Dœllinger had pointedly, refused assent. The Archbishop furthermore states that the Doctor had writen to him, under date March 29, 1871, causing, also, a copy of the same letter to be printed, March 31, 1871, in the columns of the *Allgemeine Zeitung*, of Augsburg.

The communication to the Archbishop, and to the public, through the medium of a newspaper, sets forth, and gives world-wide publicity to the reasons...the only reasons...alleged by Herr Von Dœllinger for refusing assent to the defined dogma of Papal Infallibility. We give the alleged reasons, reducing them into the form of four distinct propositions. It is easily understood, from the above explanation, that the objected propositions must be regarded, not as if taken at random from circulating gossip, or from newspaper reports, but, as being the true, official, declaration of the grounds upon which

Cæsar's friend, in the Bavarian university, has been pleased to threaten secession from the one fold of the one shepherd. The four objected propositions from the authentic orginal manifesto of Ignatz Von Dœllinger, D. D., are these, to wit:...

1. The doctrine of Papal Infallibility, as defined and decreed July 18, 1870, is not in accordance with the Holy Scriptures, as understood by the Fathers of the Church."

2. The doctrine of Papal Infallibility is not in accordance with the writings of the Fathers of the Church, which have been handed down to our times, according to their true history.

3. The question of Papal Infallibility, as defined and decreed July 18, 1870, is a purely historical question, which ought to be resolved, solely, by the same means, and rules, which apply to any other historical fact, and, *Analytical Treatment of History* demonstrates historical facts which flatly contradict the doctrine of an Infallible Pope.

4. The definition and decree of July 18, 1870, concerning Papal Infallibility are in contradiction with the constitutions of European States, and, particularly, with that of Bavaria. This belief wrought the ruin of the old German Empire, and, if suffered to prevail with the Roman Catholic portion of the German nation, it will plant the germs of a lingering and incurable malady in the constitution of the new Empire."

The venerable, learned, and patrotic Archbishop of Munich repudiates, with loudly expressed disgust, the sly insinuations of contrariety between Catholic faith and German constitutions. The indignant prelate breaks forth in these words:..."Against this erroneous theory and hateful accusation we protest with a loud voice, and

declare it an unfounded charge against the Catholic
Church, her Head, her Bishops, and all her members,
who will never cease to "give unto Cæsar that which is
Cæsar's." Universal Christendom re-echoes the Archbishop's declarative protest.

Reader dear, the learned Dr. Dœllinger proclaims
that "Analytical Treatment of History" is just the
˅ plan of plans," whereby one can arrive at a true
knowledge of things to be believed. The fourth proposition, given above, may be considered as the starting
base of the "new departure." Suppose we try to measure that starting base, by a little application of "analytical treatment." To this writer's mind, the fourth
proposition suggests the true and only inducing cause of
the whole Bavarian movement, to wit:...Cæsar, first...
God, next. That proposition clearly decrees in this
manner:..."Do not obey God's commandments until
you are made certain, from '*Analytical treatment of
history*,' that the things which God commands are not in
contradiction with the constitutions of European States,
but, particularly, make sure that the commanded things
are not in contradiction with the constitution of Bavaria.' Be vigilant, lest Almighty God may 'plant the
germs of a lingering and incurable malady in the constitution of the new German Empire,' to which belong our
first love, and our exclusive allegiance."

"The doctrine of Papal Infallibility is an innovation,"
exclaims Dr. Dœllinger. "Papal Infallibility is a novelty,
...an article of belief never recognized, never thought of,
in the Catholic Church, until July 18, 1870," cry out a
few designing clackers in the back ground, to whom
"the old man of seventy odd" is foolish enough to lend
himself for the purpose of pawing-out warm chestnuts
for the interested and crafty coterie.

"If that new article of belief is suffered to prevail it will destroy the *new*, in like manner as, formerly, it certainly wrought the ruin of the *old*, German Empire!" shout forth stentorian lungs from so-called evangelical pulpits.

"Good gentlemen, all, how so? How does it appear that the new article of belief must inevitably bring about the ruin of the new Empire?"

"The distinguished Herr Von Dœllinger, of *ours*, can prove the facts from 'Analytical Treatment of History!'" is the only reply from coterie or pulpit.

Well! well! we must ask an explanation from "*their* most learned man in all Germany." How is it, Doctor?

"My objected proporsitions, furnished to the ecclesiastical authorities through the Archbishop of Munich, and to the world at large through the cloumns of the *Allgemeine Zeitung*, are worded plainly enough. Read them. The new belief is 'in contradiction with' the constitution of the new Empire, and that innovated article of faith will plant in that constitution the germ of a lingering and incurable malady."

"But, Doctor! Herod of Sardinia has had Pius IX in prison from a date preceding the beginning of your new German Empire. As yet, we notice no conflict between the new article of faith and the constitution of the new Empire. How can the two things be declared 'in contradiction with each other,' since there has never been any practical contact in their respective operations? Why give the 'new belief' a bad name, all at once, without even the semblance of a trial?"

"This very, article of belief," exclaims the learned Professor of history, "this very article of belief wrought the ruin of the *old*, and of course, if suffered to prevail, what can we expect but that it will be a principle of destruction to the *new*, German Empire?"

That new article of belief, so recently thought of, and.
so lately added to the *credenda*, will be the ruin of
Bavaria, and. likewise, of the new German Empire!
Why? Because Herr Von Dœllinger has professed history for half a century, and his profound learning has
found out as follows, to wit:...Papal Infallibility is a
new article of belief which, never before, was believed in
Christendom, as all history most clearly demonstrates!
If the new belief be suffered to prevail in Germany, it
will surely subvert the constitution of the new Empire,
as past experience has manifested! This novelty ot faith,
which *never* was believed, is the same old belief which,
long ago, *was* the prevailing strong belief throughout all
Germany, and that, too, at a time when, as yet, nobody
in the whole world had so much as thought about the
point in the light of an article of belief! A thing that
never existed, did, because it always existed. ruin the old
Empire, which had co-existed with Papal Infallibility
for nearly a thousand years.

But, forsooth, is it not clearly apparent from history
that it was the Pope who ruined the old Empire! Is it
not a fact of history that the first Napoleon kept the Pope
a close prisoner whilst he was hammering the old Empire
into fragments? And is it not plainly evident from history that the Pope was retained a close prisoner because
the Corsican despot could neither coax nor compel the
good old Holy Father to give aid or comfort to the
usurping scoundrel who did ruin and annihilate the once
famous "Holy Roman Empire?" Now, after so clear an
elucidation, who can doubt that " Papal Infallibility "
will prove a sore trial to the new Imperial Government?
If so terrific when it *was not*,...now that *it is*, what may
we not expect?

Friendly reader, please, once more, glance over the

four propositions of Doctor Dœllinger, and gather from them, if you can, a plainer Anglo-Saxon synopsis of "whys" and "wherefores" than your humble servant has been able to do. For his own part, he, now more than ever, feels the loss of having been deprived, in his earlier years, of all the advantages derivable from Bavarian mataphysics of history. Herr Von Dœllinger is not a young man, an ignorant man, nor a fool. He has put forth four propositions as alleged reasons for not hearing the church. This writer cannot fathom the full force of the Doctor's words and expressions, but he can guess at their general meaning. He presumes the great analyzer of history desires to insinuate as follows:...

"Jesus Christ established an Infallible Church; all men are commanded to hear that church under penalty of damnation for refusal; the commandments of Christ and the glaring crimes or despotic passions of European rulers are not seldom at variance. Cæsar fain would have the commandments of Christ a dead letter. In so far as said commandments may be applicable to European kings or cabinets, they try to render the commandments a completely dead letter; and the last state of those men becomes worse than the first. Now, Doctor Dœllinger argues that all these perplexities of Cæsar and subordinate rulers could have been avoided, if only, when the Catholic Church was founded, Jesus Christ had taken a little more precaution about the future...if only Christ our Lord had foreseen things more clearly, and had not given to His Church an organization and a constitution which, some day or other, might prove to be "in contradiction with" the constitutions of European States, but particularly "in contradiction with" that of dear old Bavaria.

Alas, poor Dœllinger! Alas, thy treatment of history!

CHAPTER THIRD.

VI.

That fine old American gentleman familiarly known by the *sobriquet* "Unabridged," defines the word *define*.

The term means:..."To determine with precision; to make out with exactness; to ascertain or exhibit clearly; to explain." Noah Webster defined that word; he did not make it.

It does seem strange that so many apparently well informed non-Catholics find themselves unable to discern the difference between defining an article of faith and making one. How readily the same good folk can appreciate the distinction between defining a word and making that word. The Catholic church never has defined...never can define...a *new* article of faith. The charter of divine commission given to her from the Eternal Father, by the Eternal Son, *St. Matthew* xxviii, 18, 19, 20, and *St. Mark* xvi, 15, 16; the instructions from Jesus himself, *St. Matthew* xvii, 17; and the plain corollaries of St. Paul, *Galatians* i, 8, and I *Timothy* vi, 20; leave no room for uncertainty as to the limits of her God-received jurisdiction for legislative purposes, and for the spiritual government of all men. Every one who is a descendant of Adam must hear the voice of the teaching church when that voice reaches him, or else he will be damned. King James' version has that strong word fully displayed, *St. Mark*, xvi, 16. There is no alternative. The message is from God Himself; St. Paul wrote it down; the unchallenged documents are in our hands; we know that Holy church only delivers what she has received. She never innovates in teaching the true faith. Councils sanctioned by Popes, and Popes without councils, wherever time and circumstances seemed to demand, have often defined *anew*, this or that point of the ancient faith, but neither council nor Pope ever did, or ever could define a new article of Catholic Faith. Definitions have always been made for the purpose of *keeping out*, and not for the purpose of *bringing in*, something new. "To exhibit clearly," "to explain" what has been handed down from the beginning, does not *bring in*,...but it does *keep out*,...all strange doctrines which are not of God. Arius would innovate, and the church defined; Luther and Co. would innovate, and the church defined; the church, quite lately; influenced by the Holy Ghost, has defined *anew* concerning an *old* article of faith, and now, Herr Von Dœllinger and Co. are trying their best to innovate.

Reader dear, do you not readily perceive the self-evident difference between defining *anew*, an old article of faith, and defining a *new* article. With Holy Scriptures, and truthful records of nearly nineteen hundred years, spread open under our very eyes, men like Arius, and Luther, and Dœllinger, would fain cover their own innovating pranks by raising the alarming cry, "innovation!" against some needed and called-for Papal definition. A sensible detective was he, and filled with knowledge of human nature, who, in a crowded thoroughfare, when the cry "stop thief" was raised, nabbed without ceremony the foremost thief hunter whose shouts were first, fiercest, and most frequent. That detective made no mistake in picking out his man.

A cry against the Catholic Church, charging her with innovating upon the faith once delivered to the Saints," *St. Jude*, 3....and the cry proceeding from most outrageous would-be innovators...is decidedly rich. For almost two thousand years our church has marked all innovators and kept them out side her pale. *Rom.* xvi, 17. With infallible fidelity she has kept that which was committed to her trust. I *Tim.* vi, 20. And the things which she heard from Jesus and the Apostles she commended to faithful men, fit to teach others. 2. *Tim.* ii, 2. And, as to faith, organization, government, constitution, authority to teach, with corresponding obligation of all men to hear and to obey, our Catholic Church under Pius IX, is that same Unit which Paul and Barnabas preached, and which Peter governed. Dœllinger, Luther, Arius, *et hoc genus omne*, in attempting to force "novelties" upon Christendom, to the detriment of the true and entire faith received from Christ and the Apostles, have occupied themselves in a sort of business concerning which we are assured that, were even an angel from heaven to occupy himself in the same kind of business, such an angel would be deseving of hell. St. Paul is our authority for the assertion, and Paul had it from Christ. *Galatians* i, 1 and 8.

VII.

THE TERM "INFALLIBILITY" DEFINED.

Infallibility, as the word is used and understood by the Catholic Church, has a fixed and precise signification. Infallibility means:—AN ABSOLUTELY CERTAIN AND TRUE DECLARATION OF WHAT GOD HAS REVEALED.

Infallibility of the Church means that, according to the promises of God, and under the guiding influence of the Holy Ghost, the Church cannot teach to men any doctrinal point, as of obligation to be believed, except what God Himself has revealed.

Papal Infallibility means an absolute exemption from liability to error in teaching what God has revealed, which exemption from error comes from God *to* the Church, *through* one certain, divinely-appointed, official, ministerial channel. That official ministerial channel is the successor of St. Peter, the Supreme Head, on earth, of the Universal Church, the Bishop of Rome, commonly called...the Pope. There can be no mental difficulty in fully comprehending what a Catholic means when he uses the term "Infallibility," or the expression "Papal Infallibility." It does not mean "impeccability," or exemption from liability to displease God by personal sin. The Pope is a man like other men. He goes to confession and performs the penance enjoined by the priest, just as every other practical Catholic who tries to keep himself, by grace, in the friendship of God. Human weaknesses of conduct in the affairs of life do not lessen the prerogative of "Infallibility" divinely attached to the executive and judicial Headship of the Church.

Our esteemed friend "Average," from his platform of ignorance, "goes on dreadfully" about impious pretensions that a man can be "infallible," whereas the Scriptures declare that if any man says he is without sin, the truth is not in him. I *St. John*, i, 8. His catholic neighbor has tried his best to make the poor fool understand the difference between "impeccability" and "infallibility." "Catholic" has told "Average," a thousand times, that "the cause why a Papal difinition concerning Faith and Morals is infallible, lies not in the person of the Pope, but in the divine assistance of the Holy Ghost, by whose power the Church is preserved from every lapse into error. Friend " C." tells friend "A." that a man, without being impeccable or sinless, can be so protected by the power of God that he cannot, officially, teach any doctrine in God's name which God did not commission him to teach. The earnest "C." thinks that one must be an infallible blockhead...giving true and certain evidence of blockheadism--who tries to understand but cannot, that God may commission a man, and endow that man with plenipotentiary prerogatives to make known the "Divine Law," and to expound the same, without liability to error in any particular regarding the trust...whilst, at the same time, that same man may not be pleasing to God in all things. A believer and a reader of Holy Bible can be at no loss for an illustration as to the point which "C." would define into the knowledge receptacle which poor "A." is supposed to possess. Here is an illustrative little narrative :

After the going out from Egypt, Moses was the divinely appointed leader of God's poeple, and the Head of the Jewish nation, during forty years. He received "the Law" and delivered it to the people. In his official position, during that forty years, Moses was "a true and certain" deliverer of God's revelation, and "a true and certain" expounder of the exact meaning of the said revelation. One cannot be a believer of divine revelation who does not acknowledge that Moses was a divinely-constituted, inerrable teacher of God's people from the Exodus until his death. During all this time Moses was gifted from God with personal "infallibility." Deny the fact, and the truth of the Bible and of all revelation is likewise denied.

Was Moses also impeccable during all that number of years, as a consequence of his personal infallibility ?

Let the God of Moses give the answer. Read *Deuter-onomy* i and xxxii, and *Numbers* xxvii. Said God to Moses: "Go up into mount Nebo, and die thou in the mountain, because thou trespassed against me in the midst of the Children of Israel, and thou didst not sanctify my name among the Children of Israel." "Thou shalt see the land before thee which I will give to the Children of Israel, but thou shalt not enter into it."

Moses, during a long career of official duties, was gifted with personal infallibility...he was not impeccable. Long before the end of his official term he had trespassed against God in the midst of the Children of Israel, not by teaching error, against which he was God-protected, but by some personal misconduct. And Moses, the servant of God, an "Infallible" teacher and an "Infallible" writer of God's revelation, continuing to be, for many subsequent years, such a teacher and such a writer, had been all the while under the decreed sentence of God, that he might look at the land of promise from the summit of Mount Nebo, but that, for some personal sin during his official administration, he should set foot upon the soil of the promised inherit-ance--never!

Reader, is it hard to understand how, if God so wills it, a man may be infallible in teaching God's com-mandments, without being, as a necessary consequence, beyond personal reproach?

VIII.

A MISCHIEVOUS LOGOMACHY SETTLED.

How does it happen that many non-Catholics of the best intentions cannot bring their minds to bear with clearness upon the Catholic doctrine of Papal Infalli-bility? We will try to explain.

In former days of the English language, when it was a matter of being hung, drawn, and quartered, if a Catholic dared to teach his child to read or decipher the Alphabet, there was, in England, a man called an "Anglican Prelate," by name "Tillotson." He was a learned man for those times,...a great preacher, and, withal, a staunch hater of Popery. He used to write and preach fiercely against the Catholic Church, and, particularly, he liked to "pitch in" against Infallibility. He fancied, as Bavarian courtiers do now, that the more prejudice could be created against the dogma, so much the better could a point be made to aid and comfort the cause of "his most sacred majesty," who used to say that he ruled "by the grace of God." Now, Tillotson knew very well that he could not make "a hard blow at the papacy," on that point, if it should be clearly understood what Catholics did really mean by the term Infallibility. Then, as now, it was no hard task to misrepresent any thing Catholic, for there existed no facilities of access to sources of correct information. Men were then beginning to make dictionaries as we now have them. Thinks Tillotson to himself, " I will fix an odious meaning to the word 'Infallibility,' and it will be a splendid point against the Papacy." He succeeded. The odious meaning...anti-Catholic meaning...has been dictionaried, and school-booked into the public mind, for generations past, in England and her former colonies, so that a Catholic and a Protestant are far from attaching the same idea to that one same word. A Catholic knows that in deriving the word from Greek, through Latin and French, or whatever other way one may bring the word into the English vocabulary, "incapability of telling what is not true" is the true idea which the word suggests.

Average Protestant has been public-schooled into an acceptation of a meaning to the word which no French- man, ancient Roman or Greek could recognize.

Let us see how the "Logomachy" works. "Catholic" and "Average" are at the question of "Infallibility" again. It never has occurred to either to enquire what the other means when the word is used. "Average" wonders how "Catholic" can be such a fool as to believe so absurd and so impossible a dogma as the so much talked-of Infallibility of the Pope, or of any one else on earth. "Catholic" is filled with amazement mingled with disgust that "Average" cannot see the reasonable- ness and verisimilitude of the dogma, even if he does not believe it. "Average" is ready to swear to the fact that Moses and the High Priests of the Jewish Church delivered an absolutely true and certain declaration of what God revealed "A." is willing to take his Bible oath that all the Apostles did the same. "C." can see no difficulty in beliving in like manner concerning the Head on earth of the Christian Church, provided it be proved that God made a promise to that effect and kept his promise...a matter of fact which must be proved as other facts. For the life of him "Catholic" cannot conceive the reason why "Average" works his ears forward and backward with so much furious rapidity at the very sound of the Catholic teaching concerning Papal Infallibility. It is easily observed that "C." speaks of one thing whilst "A." thinks of another. "C." has the common sense idea of the word; "A." took his outrageous notion about the word from the dictionary, wherein that word, in English, in bitterest anti-Catholic days, was inserted and defined for a purpose. Reader, turn to the word as given by our own "Unabridged" Noah Webster: "INFALLIBILITY, *the quality of being In-*

fallible." That definition is as clear as any man in Holland could give the meaning; and that definition is Noah's own, copy-righted, we presume! Then follows the everlasting illustration of Tillotson : ..."INFALLIBILITY is *the highest perfection of the knowing faculty.*"...God bless us! "The highest perfection of the knowing faculty! Whenever did God give to mere man, or promise to give, that "highest perfection of the knowing faculty?" What Catholic ever said or thought that when St. Paul delivered to other faithful men "a true and certain" statement of truths which Jesus Christ commissoned him to teach, he, the said St. Paul, was possessed of the highest perfection that can be predicated of God alone! St. Paul was infallible in delivering God's Holy Law, because God made him so; but he was not omniscient, because his mission from heaven was to teach the doctrines of revelation...not the deductions of science.

Now, is it any wonder that "Average" thinks "Catholic" a simpleton for believing that every Pope, from the fact of being Pope, is gifted with "the highest perfection of the knowing faculty." Is it wonderful that, in turn, "Catholic" regards "Average" as little better than an innocent ninny for giving such a far-fetched meaning to so plain a word,...particularly when the far-fetched meaning was fixed to the word by an Anglican bigot for no other purpose than that the fixed meaning might serve as a handle to a hammer wherewith to rap at Popery? It is easy to perceive, then, why it is that, in our days, most generally, a Catholic and a Protesant do not speak or write about the question of Infallibility from the same stand point of a fixed idea.

"Highest perfection of the knowing faculty" is the Protestant *false idea* of Infallibility. That perfection, certainly, was never given or promised to any mere man.

An absolutely certain and true declaration of what God has revealed is the Catholic *true idea* of Infallibility. That prerogative certainly was promised and given by Almighty God, at sundry times and in divers manners to men, for man's enlightenment. *Heb.* i, 1. Friendly reader, do you experience the least difficulty in comprehending the explanation of the word "Infallibility?" The writer thinks that every one, who, for a few minutes, will ponder the sentences which he has written, must confess no difficulty in admitting that the Catholic dogma is neither an absurdity nor an impossibility, but, rather, something bearing the appearance of a verisimilitude.

Amend thy big dictionary, O great "Unabridged!" *"Highest perfection of the knowing faculty!"* what a definition of the plain word *infallibility!* The French, Spanish, Portuguese, Italian, and other modern languages, have the word in its proper signification from the positive Greek term *Phallo*, and positive Latin *Fallo*, meaning, properly, *I make to fall;* the negative conveying the idea, *I make to* NOT *fall*, or, *incapacity to deceive.* In the English language, alone, an absurd definition is attached to the word. We have explained the "reason why."

These things being so, let us enter upon a brief examination of the question of questions. Did God give Infallibility to men for the benefit of man? If God did give that high prerogative for our benefit and enlightenment, where, on earth, shall we find it? The question is quite interesting and extremely important.

CHAPTER FOURTH.

IX.

THE SOLID FOUNDATION OF OUR FAITH.

When a child is born to Catholic parents it is, at the earliest moment, baptized into the one body of Christ's Church. i *Gor.* xii. 13. When reason begins to dawn, its first turning, by the care of a pious mother, is directed toward God. Mother teaches the little one how to make the sign of the cross, and explains what that signing of the cross means. Mother's example and teaching lead reason, as its capacities expand, to a right use of itself in considering "questions of the soul." What Catholic does not often call back to recollection his days of innocence when he used to "get by heart," and used to try his best not to forget, the nice and short but full-of-meaning answers to the important questions... "Which must we take the most care of, our body or our soul?" "What must we do to save our souls?" "How shall we know the things which we are to believe?" The answer to the last question is always a perfect "settler," for the time being, as to a Catholic young gentleman's rule of faith. He is convinced that the knowledge of things that he must believe is to be sought "from the Catholic Church of God which He has appointed to teach *all* nations all those things which He has revealed." The grace of God received in Baptism makes it easy for human reason to make a right use of itself by submitting to the guidance of what it judges to be competent authority. Thus the grace of God, the right use of human reason, and competent authority, lead the Catholic child onward to fullness of divine faith, and to Catholic practical duties of life.

In time, human reason acquires plenitude of its natural development. Habitual and actual graces strengthen the native powers of reason, enabling it to go on still forward in making a right use of its God-given noble prerogatives...directing it to search for the foundation of that authority which, yet, continues to demand submission to its guidance. Corresponding to God's sufficient grace, which is denied to no one, a Catholic, by right use of his reason, is led to know that the "Light of Reason," if he who reasons be a sincere and candid searcher for God's truth, must lead, by direct process of reasoning, straight forward into the Holy Catholic Church. The Catholic child is now a full-grown adult, capable of employing all the powers of enlightened and noble "Reason." Reader dear, let us examine by what process human reason brings adults to the point of believing in Jesus Christ. Perhaps the case of the Samaritans, *St. John* iv, may not be considered an inappropriate illustration. "Now of that city many of the Samaritans believed in him for the word of the woman giving testimony. So when the Samaritans were come to him, they desired him that he would tarry there. And he abode there two days. And many more believed in him. And they said to the woman: "We now believe, not for thy saying; for we ourselves have heard him, and know that this is indeed the Saviour of the world." Thus it is with a Catholic. At first, grace strengthening reason, the young believer regards the testimony of what is considered competent authority as a sure foundation of faith. Subsequently, Reason, which in the beginning believed "for the word of the woman giving testimony," afterward says to the woman, "I now believe, not for thy saying," for I myself have examined and heard, and know that this is indeed the necessary, and the only true faith. In order to facilitate a clear understanding of the process by which enlightened *human reason* leads to the Catholic church, the writer will take the liberty of selecting and arranging, with only a slight variation of a word now and then, a page or two of paragraphs selected from an able letter addressed, A. D. 1825, to a correspondent under the *nom de plume* "Truth," by the Rt. Rev. first Bishop of Charleston, Dr. John England. We will begin the distinguished prelate's paragraphs under a separate caption as follows:...

X.

REASON DEMONSTRATES THE CATHOLIC CHURCH.

OUR FIRST PRINCIPLE is that man is not bound to believe any doctrine as of divine truth, unless that doctrine has been revealed by God. A Catholic does not acknowledge any power, or right, in the Church, nor in any portion thereof, nor in any angel, nor in any being except God Himself, to require his belief of a doctrine which is above his reason's discovery. When a Catholic says that the Church is infallible in giving her doctrinal decisions, he does not mean to say that she can make that which God did not reveal become an article of Faith. He does not mean that she can add to the revelations of God and be infallibly correct in making the addition.

But, man *is* bound to believe what God teaches. The light of Reason, that noblest gift of God to man, suggests...tells plainly...that man is bound to believe what God teaches. Yet, as man is a being endowed with *Reason*, he must have a sufficient motive for his assent or belief; in other words, he is not required to believe without evidence. Thus, for Faith evidence is necessary, otherwise man's belief would have no foundation upon which it could rest.

Now, what evidence is required? Certainly, if Reason could discover the truth of the doctrine submitted to the mind, it would be quite superfluous for God to teach what we could discover without His teaching. If we did discover the truth of the doctrine submitted to the mind, without the teaching of God, and, *solely*, by the exertion of our own intellect, our belief would be founded upon the evidence of Reason, and further evidence would be superfluous. But if the intellect did not make the discovery by its own exertion,...if no exertion of the human mind could reach so far,...and if there was furnished to it sufficient testimony of the truth *from* some person who had *seen* and *known*, and who had *testified;*... and, moreover, if the witness who had seen, and known, and testified, was known and recognized as being ONE who could neither deceive nor be deceived,...then this testimony would be, to the mind, sufficient evidence of the truth of the doctrine. Belief would then be founded upon evidence, or as the expression is, upon authority. But the mind requires still further evidence. It requires evidence that *such a witness* did give *such testimony*. That evidence would be a sure foundation of Faith. Belief then would be reasonable. God is such a witness. His vision and His knowledge are unbounded, and His testimony must be received as undoubted,...as certain assurance of fact,...unalterable testimony. Whatever He once asserts for truth will be truth forever.

These principles are manifestly true. We now come to matter of fact and deduction. God did reveal His knowledge. They to whom He revealed it had evidence of the fact. They were bound. Why? Because they had an Infallible certainty...that the Lord spoke, and an Infallible certainty of what He said. Thus, with regard to doctrines of Faith, the principle which obligates men to belief is founded in the Infallible certainty of God's declaration.

From this we perceive the indissoluble connection of Faith with an Infallible certainty of truth. Take away the certainty, upon what will Faith rest? Give the *Infallibility*, we see the basis of Faith. Conjecture is not Faith. Probability is not Faith. FAITH IS CERTAIN KNOWLEDGE RESTING UPON THE TESTIMONY OF GOD. Faith must be founded upon an Infallible certainty that God made a revelation,...and upon an Infallible certainty of what that revelation was. Thus we have a correct view of what the Catholic Church teaches concerning Faith, namely:...that when God required man to believe doctrines upon His testimony, He furnished man with an Infallible mode of knowing, exactly, what man was to believe: in other words, He gave to man *evidence*, as the foundation upon which his faith should rest. Indeed, if God did not furnish man with an Infallible *guide*, it would be unreasonable to make Faith necessary for salvation.

XI.

PRACTICAL APPLICATION OF OUR FIRST PRINCIPLE.

Candid reader, the preceding section gives sound Catholic doctrine. It is not hard to understand "our first principle." Let us hasten onward and discover to what practical results that "first principle" may lead us. We will begin thus:

"Without faith it is impossible to please God." *Heb.* xi, 6. If Faith be necessary for salvation an Infallible guide is absolutely necessary. Human reason, of its own native light, sees and admits the necessity. Faith was necessary so soon as God spoke to man. God made promises and declarations to Adam. Promises and declarations were made to Adam's Children...sometimes by special revelation from God Himself, sometimes by *other* testimony. Those testimonies were not written. God did not reveal them, specially, to each individual; yet these persons had faith founded upon these promises and declarations, and, concerning them, they had abundant evidence to create an Infallible certainty. There was no public tribunal, but there was public testimony as to the special facts. And, there was special, and renewed, and frequent, revelation to a well known public character whose communication with God was matter of public and important notoriety. Thus, from the days of Adam to the days of Moses, no generation passed away without such evidence; and this evidence gave Infallible certainty of what God told man. Thus, man was not left to conjecture, to opinion, or to probability. He had always an Infallible witness, ...a witness who could not deceive him. Upon this he believed with certainty. This was Faith which pleased God. Infallibility, then, is no novelty, as every reader can plainly see.

After the Exodus, the chosen people gathered at Sinai had, there as well as before, undoubted evidence that God spoke to Moses and commissioned him to write the Almighty's communication. God, again and again, gave most striking evidence that the writing contained the

communication of His divine will. By the direction
of God Himself "a tribunal of last resort" was established among the Children of Israel to perpetuate "a
true and certain declaration" of what the Omnipotent
had revealed...AN INFALLIBLE TRIBUNAL.

Were there, to us, no other mode of conviction as to
facts in the case, "Analytical Treatment of History,"
which the Bavarian head of the "new departure" sets
up as most worshipful assurance of certainty of past
facts, shows forth most faithfully in evidence of our
stated position. Here is a little specimen of our mode
of "Analytical Treatment:"...

Before the law was given at Sinai Moses had received
the evidence of God's revelation by the tradition of his
nation. He had, also, several special revelations. His
authority had been attested by *evident* miracles, and he
was, now, at the mountain where a further revelation
was to be made in presence of the people. We know
that, before this period,...before the written law...ques-
tions must have arisen concerning the "Law of God"
and the interpretation thereof. How were these questions decided? *Exodus* xviii furnishes an answer to the
query. Moses sat to judge the people, who stood by
him from morning until night. Says Moses to his in-
quiring kinsman, Jethro: "When any controversy fall-
eth out among them, they come to me to judge between
them, and to show the precepts of God and His laws."
Moses appointed able men to judge lesser matters only,
but "when any great matter soever fell out, and whatsoever was of greater difficulty they referred to him,"
and "Moses alone was to the people in those things
that pertain to God." That was the plan of God for
security against doctrinal error among His chosen people before the arrival at Sinai. There was a living.

present, speaking, Infallible expounder of God's revealed doctrines..."a tribunal of last resort," from the decisions of which there was no appeal. And all this by God's own appointment, even before the establishment of the Church and written positive religion of the Jews. It was the plan of God that, subsequently, a *more perfectly* organized teaching church of prefiguration, with a *more distinctly recognizable* "tribunal of last resort," should commence and date from Moses on Mount Sinai. It was the plan of God that, ultimately, a *most perfectly* organized teaching church of the reality, with a *most distinctly* recognizable "tribunal of last resort," should have a beginning from Jesus Christ on the hill of Calvary. O dear! O dear! "Analytical Treatment of History" shows rank popery developing itself all along the line of ages, among God's people, from earliest hours of Adam's primeval transgression, even until this day of Pius the Great and the Vatican Council! and the "treatment" exhibits God Himself, and none other, as the OMNIPOTENT, OMNISCIENT DEVELOPER! Let us hasten down the stream of time.

From Adam to Noah, from Noah to Abraham, from Abraham to Moses, God's people, through God's protecting care, have had, always, an Infallible human witness of what God commanded to be believed and practiced in order to salvation. Now, about fifteen hundred years before Christianity, the Children of Israel have an organized church. It is unnecessary to dwell upon details. The writer will only exhibit from "the documents" the divinely established "tribunal of last resort," figurative of what was to be more perfectly manifested in the future most perfect Church of Jesus Christ. "Analytical treatment" of *Deuteronomy* xvii gives this result:..."If thou perceive that there be among you a hard and doubtful matter in judgment, arise and go up to the place which the Lord thy God shall choose, and thou shalt come to the judge that shall be at that time, and thou shalt ask the truth of the judgment. And thou shalt do whatsoever they shall say that preside in the place which the Lord shall choose, and what they shall teach thee. Thou shalt neither decline to the right hand nor to the left hand. But he that will be proud, and refuse to obey the commandment of the priest who ministereth at the time to the Lord thy God, and the decree of the judge, that man shall die, and thou shalt take away the evil from Israel."

The High Priest of the Jews was appointed by Almighty God Himself, and derived his authority immediately from heaven. He was "a tribunal of last resort." Conspicuous upon his breastplate were *Urim* and *Thummim*, words signifying *Illuminations* and *Perfections*, which we translate *doctrine* and *Truth*, *Exodus* xxviii, 30; for God had appointed him the judge to decide, and the witness to testify the true doctrines which God had revealed. All historians of the nation concur with Josephus and Philo that the High Priests of the Jews were their judges of controversy, whose authority was not only respectable, but ultimate and conclusive, binding upon every man in Israel. This authority was theirs by virtue of their office. It sometimes happened that a High Priest was none of the best of men. The case was so in the days of the Redeemer. Jesus Himself refers to them and to their authority. It was before the *consummatum est* of Redemption, before the Jewish Church became superseded. Jesus said to the multitude and to his disciples, speaking of those who were the chief priests and rulers: "They sit in the chair of Moses. All things, *therefore*, whatsoever they shall say to you observe and do, but according to their works do ye not." *St. Matth.* xxiii, 23. Could any one manifest or recommend greater respect for authority than did our dear Lord, though the authority had fallen into very indifferent hands, and drew near the term of its limitation. Jesus tells us the doctrinal teaching of the Jewish High Priest was Infallible. He could not teach error. The Saviour talked plainly to the point; but there is no hint about "highest perfection of the knowing faculty," or about an imagined inseparable union between Infallibility and Sinlessnes. No wonder that, now and then, the ideas of poor "Average" get bewildered. He would stick to his "cue," but he hates to "go back on" the Bible! He cannot cling to both.

XII.

EXODUS OF THE JEWISH—ADVENT OF THE CHRISTIAN CHURCH.

It was a glorious Church of the figure, that old Church of God among the Jews, although it, and its authority, had to do with a stiff-necked, hard-hearted, and hard-headed people. In the fullness of time it was to be succeeded by a most glorious, permanent, and unalterable Church of the reality, concerning which the Prophets chanted forth, in splendid imagery, though in plainest words. Hear the holy seers sounding forth their God-inspired illuminations respecting the future Church of Christ. That Church is promised. The time of its advent is clearly declared. It is to be a Church most perfect. In all its doctrinal teachings there must be Infallibility for the benefit and enlightenment of men. It is not even imaginable that God, toward the Christian Church, could have less careful solicitude about furnishing "a true and certain assurance" regarding his revealed doctrines than he had always manifested during the continuance of the original Oral, and subsequent Mosaic, dispensations. What kind of a Church of the new dispensation was to succeed the Mosaic? Let us hearken to the sublime communications of the inspired Prophets that we may examine and judge if the reality be in accordance with the promises. Here are a few characteristics of what Christ's Catholic Church on earth was announced to be,...characteristics which, of course, that Church must have always manifested clearly to the world from the days of Christ, and must always continue to manifest :

"In the days of those kingdoms the God of heaven will set up a kingdom that shall never be destroyed; and his kingdom shall not be delivered up to another people; and it shall break in pieces, and shall consume all these kingdoms: and itself shall stand forever." *Daniel* ii, 44.

"And in the last days, the mountain of the house of the Lord shall be prepared on the top of mountains ; and it shall be exalted above the hills; and all nations shall flow into it." *Isaias* ii, 2.

"And a path and a way shall be there, and it shall be called the holy way; the unclean shall not pass over it; and this shall be unto you a straight way, so that fools shall not err therein." *Isaias* xxxv, 8.

"He that made thee shall rule over thee. And the Redeemer shall be called the Holy One of Israel. The mountains shall be moved, and the hills shall tremble, but my mercy shall not depart from thee, and the covenant of my peace shall not be moved. And I will make thy bulwarks of jasper, and thy gates of graven stone. All thy children shall be taught of the Lord. No weapon that is formed against thee shall prosper, and every tongue that resisteth thee in judgment thou shalt condemn." *Isaias* Liv.

"I will make thee to be an everlasting glory. Thou shalt know that I am the Lord thy Saviour and thy Redeemer. Thou shalt no more have the sun for thy light by day, neither shall the brightness of the moon enlighten thee, but the Lord shall be unto thee for an everlasting light and thy God for thy glory. Thy sun shall go down no more, nor thy moon decrease, for the Lord shall be unto thee for an everlasting light, and the days of thy mourning shall be ended." *Isaias* Xi.

The sacred prophecies must needs be fulfilled to the letter. No word of the Most High shall be made void. Thus saith the Lord: "As the rain and the snow come down from heaven, and return no more thither, but soak the earth and water it and make it to spring and give seed to the sower and bread to the eater, so shall my word be which shall go forth from my mouth; it shall not return to me void, but it shall do whatever I please, and shall prosper in the things for which I sent it." *Isaias* Liii, 10, 11.

No organization calling itself the Church of Christ, and not able to make a manifest exhibit of the characteristics foretold by the prophets,...let men and societies or sects rant as they may,...can be the Church of Christ, established by Him as the only true way by which men may hope to save their souls. Let us proceed with our examination. We will soon discover that the Church foretold by the prophets and established by Jesus Christ is no other than the Holy Catholic Church, whose Supreme Head, on earth, is the Bishop of Rome, commonly called the Pope.

CHAPTER FIFTH.

XIII.

CHRIST ORGANIZES THE HOLY CATHOLIC CHURCH.

The fullness of time has come. The Redeemer is on earth. He came, not to destroy, but to perfect the law. The magnificent prophecies are to be fulfilled. The world is to have a glorious Church embracing within its jurisdiction the ends of the earth. The Church is to be built upon Unity. *Ephesians* iv. It is to be the care of God that the foundation of that unity be established, immovably and indestructibly, amidst the shifting sands of the world. If it be wondrous to observe, as we have done, the wisdom of the ways of God, in Patriarchal times, and among the chosen race of Israel, securing an ever-present, visible, speaking, Infallible Guide, so they might receive "true and certain knowledge" that God did make a revelation to man, and receive "true and certain" assurance of what God said to man, surely, under the perfected system of revelation completed by Jesus Christ, we are not to look for a less perfect organization than was given to them of old The new must needs possess, in greatest perfection, all the perfections of the preceding dispensations. He who promised and swore to fulfil was...God.

Mark the beginning of the organization of the Catholic Church! One day "Andrew findeth his brother Simon and saith to him: We have found the Messiah which is, being interpreted, the Christ. And he brought Simon

7

to Jesus. Jesus, looking upon Simon, said: Thou art
Simon son of Jona: Thou shalt be called Cephas...
ROCK. *St. John* i, 41, 42. Simon, at that time, did not
know, nor did he enquire the reason of, nor manifest
surprise at, the change of name. He had found the
Messiah, and, at the very first interview between Jesus
Christ and Simon Peter, there was a beginning of mani-
festation of the Saviour's will, and designs, and plan,
regarding the organization of the Church of the New
Dispensation.

The twelve have been called; the Apostolic College
has been formed; the Christian plan is to be further
developed. Walking, on a certain occasion, with his
disciples, Jesus halted of a sudden and said to them:
"Whom do men say that the Son of man is?" But they
said: "Some, John the Baptist, and other some Elias,
and others, Jeremias or one of the prophets." Jesus saith
to them: "But whom do you say that I am?" *St. Matth.*
xvi, 13, 14, 15. THE ROCK answered and said: "THOU
ART CHRIST THE SON OF THE LIVING GOD." That was
the first open confession, in plain words, in the face of the
world, in acknowledgment of the *Divinity* of Jesus Incarnate. The knowledge came first, *specially*, from God
to Simon. The plan of Christian organization was
developing. The reason for the change of name was
becoming manifested. Jesus answering said to him:
"Blessed art thou Simon Bar Jona; because flesh and
blood hath not revealed it to thee, but my Father who is
in heaven." (Verse 17.) Thus, we know that St. Peter
was the first to whom the Divinity of Jesus Christ was
specially revealed by the Eternal Father, and the first
to make noble and open confession of that divinity to
the world. Immediately upon this confession, another
revelation was made to Simon Peter in presence of the

disciples. The reason of the change of name was now made plain to all. As would be the action of a wise Sovereign when about to constitute a well organized army for special service, Jesus Christ the Sovereign, to those who, in due time, were to be commissioned as Chiefs of the Christian spiritual army, made known the selection of a Chief of Chiefs. The Sovereign, Jesus, then and there, pronounced His selection of sole Head to rule in the Christian organization, that His Church on earth, for ever, might continue to be ONE. The assembled disciples understood full well the Saviour's plan. A special commission was given to Peter alone. Peter's commission was of a tenor never promised to, never expected by, never given to, any follower of Jesus Christ, save to Simon Peter alone. It was befitting that the future Commander in Chief should receive from the Sovereign, in presence of the assembled, designated chiefs, a special commission defining to him and them the nature, extent, and duration of the authority and power entrusted to that Chief. Here is what the Sovereign proclaimed: "Thou art Cephas,--ROCK;--with a view to my designs, I changed thy name from Simon. Upon this Cephas,--ROCK,--I will build my Church, and the gates of hell shall not prevail against it. And I will give to THEE the keys of the kingdom of heaven. And whatsoever THOU shalt bind upon earth it shall be bound also in heaven; and, whatsoever THOU shalt loose on earth it shall be loosed also in heaven." *St. Matth.* xvi, 18, 19.

Now, therefore, we behold the Sovereign Himself, and there stands Peter, the sole designated recipient of plenitude of power, the sole designated holder of the emblematic keys, the sole designated repository of delegated plenipotentiary jurisdiction, holding special commission from the Sovereignty. How beautifully in accordance, is this plan of the Saviour, with that plan of the Omnipotent toward Moses when the Jewish Church was to be organized. "Stand thou here with ME," said God to Moses, "and I will speak to THEE all my commandments, and ceremonies, and judgments, and thou shalt teach *them* that they may do them in the land. *Deut.* v, 31. It is not hard to understand, on the occasion to which we have referred, Jesus addressing Peter, "Stand thou here with ME, and I will speak to THEE all my commandments, and thou shalt teach *them*." In the one case and in the other, God began the organization of His Church, with a view to Unity, by selecting as His own plenipotentiary representative and vicar among men...one man by whom all others were to be governed, and through whom all men were to be assured of Infallible teaching as to things of divine revelation, necessary to be believed or practised.

It was after all this that the Apostles, in a body, heard from the lips of Christ a declaration of the general commission intended for them all, "Amen I say to you, whatsoever you shall bind upon earth shall be bound also in heaven, and whatsoever you shall loose upon earth, shall be loosed also in heaven." *Matth.* xviii. 18. Already, to Peter specially, the same commission had been signified, *Matth.* xvi, 19, together with additional important powers and authority never promised to, nor expected by, either one of the eleven. To every one of them it was said: "As the Father hath sent me so I also send you." *St. John* xx, 21. All in one body received the charge: "Go ye into the whole world and preach the Gospel to every creature." *St. Mark* xvi, 15, 16. To the whole of them Jesus Christ entrusted most ample powers when He said: "All power is given to me in heaven and in earth ; go, therefore, teach ye all nations, baptizing them in the name of the Father and of the Son and of the Holy Ghost. *St. Matth.* xxviii, 18. One and all have the same general authority to teach, and their authority is immediately from Jesus Christ. They were an organized Church of which Jesus was the Supreme Head and they his commissioned teaching and governing ministers, of whom ONE was the designated Chief, with special delegated power and authority over all others. And it was the plan of God that that organization should forever be manifest and recognizable to the world, so that the glorious Church foretold by the Prophets can not fail of being always distiguishable from all other pretending societies and sects, be their names what they may.

XIV.

THE CATHOLIC CHURCH A VISIBLE FACT IN THE WORLD.

We are now at a point of time when our Church has become an organized, visible fact in the world. She is what we may call a "corporation," recognizable and recognized as such by the world at large. Being such a corporate institution, the body has a governing head, a corps of governing teachers, and, also, numbers of individual taught and governed members. Jesus has ascended from earth. The great Supreme Head of the Christian Church sitteth at the right hand of God the Father, whence He will visibly come again to judge the world. Having fully organized His Church on earth before withdrawing from it His own visible presence, it is natural that we should seek to find some open declaration of our Lord by which an assurance may be had of His plain recognition of the organization, as the same had been perfected by Himself. We shall have no difficulty in showing forth that recognition. One day, after the resurrection, in presence of the other Apostles, Jesus turned to Peter and said to him: "Simon, son of John, lovest thou me more than these?" Peter answered, "Yea, Lord, thou knowest that I love thee." Jesus said to him, "Feed my lambs." He said to him again, "Simon, son of John, lovest thou me?" He answered, "Yea, Lord, thou knowest that I love thee." Jesus said to him, "Feed my lambs." He said to him a third time, "Simon, son of John, lovest thou me?" Peter was grieved because he said to him the third time, Lovest thou me? and he answered, "Lord, thou knowest all things; thou knowest that I love thee." And Jesus said to him, "Feed my sheep." *St. John* xxi. The universal understanding of the text has been that the flock, and the pastors of the flock, were to take the food of true faith from Peter.

The situation was thoroughly understood by all who were present at the charge given by the dear Redeemer to His Chief of the Apostolic College. Not long previously the same assembly had heard from the same divine lips an address to Cephas, the Rock, which address, alone, were there no other declarations of Jesus upon the subject, ought to put to rest forever, among believers in the divinity of Jesus Christ, every question about the personal official Supremacy and Infallibility of St. Peter and his successors. It was the most solemn moment of the Saviour's earthly career. Sitting with the twelve at the last supper, He was conversing with them, giving instructions and encouragement. Suddenly He turned to one of them and said, "Simon, Simon, behold Satan hath desired to have *you* that he may sift *you* as wheat;

(mark the plural *you* referring to the assembled College;) but I have prayed for THEE that THY faith fail not, and THOU, being once converted, confirm thy brethren." *St. Luke* xxii, 31, 32. If that text is not declarative of some peculiarity of supereminence in Peter over all the others, what, then, are we to understand by the emphatic use of the *you* and the THEE which so forcibly strikes every reader of the Bible, no matter in what version, or in what language, it may be read?

It was no mere accident, nor circumstance of chance, which caused St. Matthew to say, x, 2, "The names of the twelve Apostles are these: 'The FIRST, Simon who is called Peter.'" The same order of naming is invariably observed by all the sacred writers. "The FIRST, Simon who is called Peter." The others are named in no particular order of notation, save that Judas, the Traitor, is always named the last. Whilst the Redeemer continued upon earth, a primacy of order and honor belonged to the FIRST, Simon who was called Peter. His status was recognized by the Apostolic College, as the New Testament plainly demonstrates. According to the declaration and promises of Jesus, the Son of God, plenitude of jurisdiction, and of teaching and governing authority, were to be the inalienable perogatives of Peter and his successors, after the withdrawal of Christ's visible presence from the earth. That withdrawal, and the actual beginning of Peter's plenipotentiary jurisdiction over the whole Church of Christ on earth, so far as human research can chronologize the events, may be dated, according to our present reckoning, Thursday, May 5, A. D. 29. On the day corresponding to that date of our Christian era, the whole Christian Church on earth, numbering about one hundred and twenty souls, all told, was assembled under presidency of its

Supreme Head on earth. " Peter stood up in the midst of the Apostles,". and began to exercise, for the first time, as the recognized plenipotentiary Vicar of Jesus Christ, the official prerogatives of instructing and governing. *Acts* i, 16, 22.

N. B! Even to outsiders the status of Peter and his peculiarly close official relationship to the Redeemer were known and appreciated. Is there not something remarkably to the point written by St. Matthew, xvii, 23 and 25? Public officers would collect a tax from Jesus. In the most natural way in world the Evangelist writes that the tax-man did not go to Jesus at once, nor to any other of the Saviour's followers, save to Peter. " Doth not your master pay tribute? " say the officers to Simon. Simon said to them; "yes." . And when he was come into the house Jesus anticipated him, saying: "What is thy opinion, Simon? The kings of the earth, of whom do they receive tribute or custom? of their own children or of strangers? And Simon said: Of strangers? Jesus said to him: Then the children are free. But that WE may not scandalize them, go to the sea and cast in a hook; and that fish which shall first come up, take; and when thou hast opened its mouth thou shalt find a piece of money; take that and give it to them for ME and for THEE." The text is very suggestive. The other followers of Christ, it would seem, were left to provide, each for himself, the tribute of tax-pennies.

Unchallenged exercise of an official prerogative indicates its recognized existence. The Christian Church was assembled in an upper chamber at Jerusalem. It behooved the Apostolic College to choose one to fill the vacant place of the traitor Judas. It was Peter

who rose up and proposed action in the matter. He
acted, now, officially, for the first time...the Saviour
had just ascended,...as Supreme Head on earth of the
Church of Christ; and he made the first Papal allocu-
tion, which is recorded Acts i, 16, 22.

XV.

ST. PAUL'S OFFICIAL VISIT TO ST. PETER.

To every believer in Christ St. Paul must be an acceptable witness. That great Apostle of the Gentiles
had been miraculously converted, and had received from
Jesus Christ Himself an extraordinary call to the sacred
ministry. All the Apostles and disciples who had
walked with the Lord understood, and recognized, and
appreciated, the status which St. Peter occupied toward
the Lord and toward themselves. It pleased God that
the extraordinarily converted and called St. Paul should
send down to our times unmistakable evidence that he,
also, understood, and recognized, and appreciated it.
Before entering upon the extraordinary mission of
founding Churches and calling other men to the sacred
ministry, the Apostle of the Gentiles came into the
regions of Judea. There he was "unknown by face to
the Churches which were in Christ." They had only
heard that " he who had persecuted once, now preached
the faith which he had once impugned." St. James the
Less, called the brother of the Lord, was Bishop of
Jerusalem, ever present in that City, resident there,
and of course always at home. Now, ponder the steps
which St. Paul considered it expedient for him to take
before he went about among the Churches of Judea,
and before going abroad to found new churches and or-
dain Priests and Bishops. It is no question now what

Paul might have done by virtue of the extraordinary call received directly from the Saviour Himself. It is our purpose, only, to show what Paul did do, taught as he was by divine inspiration, that no one in after ages might ignorantly allege his example for running without being sent, to preach the gospel and exercise the ministry, without first receiving recognition and authority from the divinely appointed Surpreme Head of the Church on earth, according to the orderly plan instituted by God Himself. St. Paul came from Arabia, and this is what he tells us about his course of proceding before entering upon Apostolic labors. "I went up to Jerusalem TO SEE PETER, and I tarried with him fifteen days." *Galatians* i, 17. After that visit of fifteen days the holy Paul tells in verses 17 and 21, "I came into the regions of Syria and Cilicia;" and "they glorified God in me." What a suggestive little narrative, good reader. Paul spent three years preaching in Arabia, before preparing to enter upon his grand mission of converting the Gentiles, founding Churches and ordaining ministers. Then he came into Judea, but he went not among the Churches, for they did not know his face, nor had they any evidence of his mission. They had only heard of him. But Paul knew what was to be done. He went up to Jerusalem, not to see James, the actual Bishop of that City, but he went up *to see Peter*, and to tarry with Peter for fifteen days. It was an official visit, and a long one. After seeing Peter and tarrying with him, and after having been recognized by Peter, so that the Churches knew of the visit and the tarrying, Paul came among the Churches and they glorified God in him. That was the great beginning of St. Paul's Apostolic career. How plainly the narration is given, *Galatians* i.

Just here, once for all, we will remark, in the words of St. Chrysostom, that the visit of St. Paul to St. Peter must be considered as an evidence of the high regard of Paul for the official character of Peter. "Peter," he observes, "was the organ and prince of the Apostles; on which account Paul went up to see *him* in preference to the rest." *Homily* lxxxvii, *on St. John.* Paul did not go with a view to obtain instruction, for he had been favored with a divine revelation: he entertained no doubt whatever of the correctness of his doctrine: he was equal in the Apostolic dignity to Peter; and he may have been greater in personal qualifications and merit, yet he went to see him as to a superior, honoring the office which Peter held by divine appointment. " Paul gives up to Peter as to a superior and elder, and he had no other motive for the visit, but merely to show honor to Peter and to become thorougly acquainted with him. See *St. Chrysostom on Galat.* c, i. For the edification and enlightenment of after ages St. Paul was inspired to make the visit, and to record the fact!

Modern sects affect a peculiar liking for St. Paul *because* they fancy the discovery of an inkling of Protestantism in their favorite Apostle. He, once, they imagine, had a few sharp words with St. Peter, the Pope of his day, in reference to the exhibition, on the part of the latter, of a little cowardly imprudence which touched upon neither faith nor morals. " When Cephas was come to Antioch I withstood him to the face because he was to be blamed." *Galatians* iii, 11. Admitting the fact, even the matter in question was of mere prudence and expediency of personal action,--not a question of divine truth, or of teaching of erroneous doctrine.

Nothing can be discovered in bold remonstrance such as Paul used, inconsistent with the official supremacy of him to whom it was addressed. There is one little matter of fact, however, which seems to spoil every argument which the sects try to deduce from the reproaching words of St. Paul to Cephas, in the cited text,--it remains to be proved, and it never can be proved to the satisfaction of the learned, that the Cephas whom Paul "withstood to the face," was *the* Cephas to whom the same St. Paul made an official visit of fifteen days. See *Kenrick's* "Letters on the Primacy," P. 51; and the same author's "Theologia Dogmatica," Vol. 1, p. 157.

Dear reader, it cannnot be expected that in this little book we show that Peter actually exercised one and all of the prerogatives which officially pertained to him. Besides, we have no detailed history of the Apostolic age. The *Acts of the Apostles* are confined to a few facts connected with the commencement of the Chrurch, and the conversion and chief labors of St. Paul, written by a cherished disciple and constant companion of the same St. Paul. But we have shown sufficient for our purpose. You have *the special promise* TO ST. PETER, *St. Matth.* xvi, 16, 29. You have *the special charge* TO ST. PETER, at the last Supper, *St. Luke* xxii, 31, 32. You have *the special commission* TO ST. PETER, after the resurrection, *St. John* xxi, 15, 16, 17. You cannot fail to have recognized Christ's plenipotentiary Viceroy, the Universal Superintendent and Chief Pastor of Christ's Church on earth. To use the words of the excellent Archbishop F. P. Kenrick, we show to you "Peter's commission bearing the seal of the Great King," and we demand that it be respected.

CHAPTER SIXTH.

XVI.

ST. PETER FOUNDS THE ROMAN CHURCH.

In the thirteenth year after our Lord's Ascension, in the second year of the reign of the Emperor Claudius Cæsar, A. D. 42, and tradition will have the day of, or the day after, the celebration of the anniversary of Rome's foundation, Simon Peter, Vicar on earth of Jesus Christ, Supreme Head of the Universal Christian Church, for the first time, entered the City of Rome and fixed there his permanent See. From this date he was Bishop of Rome. Christians became numerous. Converted Jews and converted Gentiles were daily added to the number of the faithful. Linus, and Cletus, and Clement, were consecrated by St. Peter, to govern the Roman Church as his deputies whilst he lived, and to inherit, as God might dispose, the succession to the Roman See and the plenitude of Peter's prerogatives, in due order of time. St. Peter remained in Rome until A. D 49. Like a skillful and good general, as St. Chrysostom expresses it, he left all things well arranged at home, and, himself, made the grand rounds, preaching everywhere, and seeing that all things were in order. He did not return to Rome, so far as known to us, until A. D. 64, and he was crucified A. D. 69, June 29, the same day on which St. Paul was beheaded, under the Emperor Nero. St. Peter governed the Uni-

versal Church after Christ's Ascension about thirty-
eight years, and he was Bishop of Rome, April, A. D.
42, June, A. D. 67, twenty-five years and five or six
weeks.

XVI.

COUNCIL OF JERUSALEM.

Whilst "making the rounds," the first Bishop of
Rome found himself at Jerusalem, A. D. 49 or 51. St.
James the Less was yet living, the resident Bishop of
that See. St Paul and St. Barnabas were actively
engaged at Antioch preaching and making converts.
Acts xv. Some brethren came down from Judea and
began to teach errors. "Paul and Barnabas had no
small controversy with them." The faithful were in
danger of receiving spiritual detriment. Paul had been
set apart by the Holy Ghost and sent upon this mission.
Acts xiii. He had, years before, gone up *to see Peter,*
and tarried with Peter fifteen days. *Galat.* i, 18. Yet
there seemed to be something lacking to him of requisite
authority, or power, to quell that disturbance at Antioch.
The faithful insisted, and St. Paul thought so, too, that
proper and prompt steps ought to be taken to crush out
the disturbances. St. Paul knew the proper mode of
proceeding. He would go up again "*to see Peter.*" Now,
all this was permitted by God for the enlightenment and
edification of after ages. St. Paul himself brought up
the appeal to the Bishop of Rome, who, by the influence
of Divine Providence, was there to receive the appeal,
and to define the faith.

St. Paul has been permitted, and even inspired, by
God to tell us the plain reason why he went up at that
time. It was God Himself who caused him to go.
Here are his own words: "After fourteen years, I went

up again to Jerusalem with Barnabas, taking Titus also with me. And I went up *according to revelation*, and conferred with *them* the gospel which I preach among the Gentiles; but *apart* with *them* who *seem* to be *something;* lest, perhaps, I *should* run, or *had* run, in vain." *Galat.* i, 1, 2.

Now, who were the *them* with whom St. Paul conferred about the gospel which he had been preaching to the Gentiles for fourteen years, and since he had tarried with Peter? And who were the other *them* who were *something*, and with whom he conferred *apart*, lest, perhaps, he had run, or should run, in vain? Clearly, to the mind of this writer, even according to private interpretation, it was another *official* visit *to see Peter.*

Let us drop in upon the council in session and observe the proceedings. Turn, dear reader, to *Acts* xv. The Apostles and ancients assembled to consider the matter. And when there had been much disputing, PETER, rising up said to them: "Men, brethren:"--then follows the decretal decision, which was afterwards committed to writing, and sent to Antioch by the hands of St. Paul and St. Barnabas; and which, also, was published throughout Syria and Cilicia. There was the end of *that* outbreak, of which nothing was heard ever afterward. In what manner was the Papal decree received by "the apostles and ancients assembled to consider the matter?" It does not appear that there was any *voting* upon the point whether or not the decision of Peter should be received by those of the council, among whom there had been "much disputing." No, indeed! It was not the plan of God, when He revealed divine truths, and commanded every man to believe them under pain of damnation, that men should *vote* by ballot, to find out by majority of votes, what men were to do in the matter. Jesus Christ did not say, Go ye and preach the Gospel to every creature, commanding *all* men to believe, and to observe, all things which I have delivered to you; but let them vote, and do not insist upon the belief of any dogma, unless you can carry a majority of *votes* in its favor. Things were not managed thus at Jerusalem. There was much disputing, that the evidences might be brought out all the more clearly by the acts of the disputants themselves. Then Peter rose up and *defined*. And when he had defined, "all the multitude held their peace. And Paul and Barnabas began to tell what great wonders God had wrought among the Gentiles by them." It was in the Episcopal See of St. James that all this took place. As yet he had said nothing, for the Pope was there and presided in person. After the decree, no one seemed to ask Paul, or James, or Barnabas what either of them thought about the decision. All the multitude held their peace. All who were in that first Christian general Council knew the revealed will of God concerning the mode divinely appointed for the preservation of *the whole depositum* of Catholic Faith. James was in his own Episcopal See. Peter was in the City of James' peculiar jurisdiction. It was brought about by God's providence that James should give a striking illustration that, though Peter was Bishop of a far distant City, and though he, (James,) was Bishop of the City, of the assembly; and though he, (James,) was the near kinsman of the Lord, yet, in the Episcopal City of James, Peter was greater in dignity, and power, and jurisdiction than was the Bishop of Jerusalem who was an Apostle even as Peter. It was proper however that, in his own See, James should be heard by his own people. "After they held their peace" James answered, saying: "Men, brethren; hear me." *What did he say to the men and brethren?* Then and there he accepted the definition, and published it, and explained the obligation which demanded compliance with all its conditions. He said *that much* and *nothing more.* Read the address of James in the text. A condensation of that address is this: "Men, brethren, Simon has declared to you the truth, and we are here as witnesses, to take the testimony, each to his respective people, and to defend it as God gives us ability." Great Apostle! it was as well known to thee as to the others of that assembly, that Peter's decree was an Infallible declaration of God's revealed truth—an Infallible declaration *so soon* as Peter rose and spoke, and *before* the expressed "placet" of any one else, present or absent.

Good reader, even until this day, the Holy Catholic Church has never permitted innovation upon the Apostolic mode of terminating, "finally and forever," all doubts and disputes about matters of divine Faith. The method displayed by the council of Jerusalem was *the* method taught by Jesus Christ. The teaching Church is Infallible in the delivery of Faith and Morals. Infallibility comes to the Church from Jesus Christ. Jesus Christ imparts that precious gift to his Church through *one* channel, and through one, *only.* That ONE channel is the successor of him to whom the God-man said, "Peter, I have prayed for *thee*, and *thou* being converted, confirm thy brethren. *St. Luke* xxii, 32.

XVII.

ST. PAUL'S TESTIMONY ABOUT THE ROMAN CHURCH.

A numerous, flourishing, and perfectly organized Christian Church, founded by St. Peter himself, began

to exist in Rome A. D. 42. Until A. D. 49 the Chief
of the Apostles, as Bishop of Rome, labored there per-
sonally, and ruled that Church without any prolonged
absence. About the latter date, the twelve thousand
Jews who were huddled together in the Jews' quarter
beyond the Tiber, became somewhat tumultuous. Very
naturally, the pagan mind did not then distinguish
between the Christian disciples and the blasphemous
Jewish hard-heads. The innocent Christians were regarded as having identical interests and feelings with
the guilty blasphemers. An order of banishment
against all Jews was issued by Claudius. *Acts* xviii, 2.
Leaving the immediate charge of Christian affairs to his
appointed deputies, St. Peter set out from Rome to
make "the grand rounds." It was during St. Peter's
absence that St. Paul who, as yet, never had visited
Rome, *wrote* to that pre-eminent Christian Church. He
wrote to that Church as never he wrote to any other.
St. Paul, years before he went to Rome, gloried in the
Faith of the Roman Church. He ardently longed to
come to them whom he called "the beloved of God,
called to be Saints." Says he to the Catholics of Rome,
"I give thanks to my God, through Jesus Christ, for
you all, because your faith is spoken of in the whole
world." *St. Paul to Romans*, i, 8. How strenuously
does he, who is regarded as a favorite Apostle by the
sects of Protestantism, insist, advise, and urge upon the
Roman Church to hold fast to the Faith which it had
received! St. Paul evidently feared no arising of schisms
among the Catholics of Rome. He spoke to them as if
there rested *there* a peculiar duty to teach and to defend
the true Faith. "I beseech you, brethren, to mark
them who cause dissensions against the doctrines which
you have learnt." *Romans* xvi, 17. That advice may

not be considered as very encouraging to dissenters. St. Paul, however, spoke very earnestly, and he spoke in God's name. All parties admit that much. None can deny that, *then*, the Church of Rome had the true faith. St. Paul, inspired of God, advised that Church to "mark them who cause dissensions" in the Christian family, and that Church of Rome has never failed to act up to St. Paul's advice. "Analytical Treatment of History" displays her holding fast to the Faith which she had received from Christ's Apostles, and marking all sowers of dissension against the doctrines which she thus learned, from that day to this, from SIMON PETER to PIO NONO.

XVIII.

THE FOURTH BISHOP OF ROME, ST. CLEMENT.

A. D. 91--100, during the life time of St. John the Evangelist, St. Clement, whose name was written in the "Book of Life," *Philip*. iv, 3, was Bishop of Rome. St. Peter was crucified June 29, A. D. 67. Previously to his death he had provided for the succession in the Church of Rome, by consecrating with his own hands St. Linus, and St. Cletus or Anacletus, and St. Clement, to succeed, each to the other, as time might determine.

St. Paul had founded the Church of Corinth. During the lifetime of the founder there happened a dissension which was noticed and reported to him by one Fortunatus, a Priest who is named with much commendation by the Great Apostle, 1 *Cor.* xvi, 17. The disturbance was quelled in a short time. Afterward, during the Pontificate of Clement, there occurred again a troublesome schism among the Corinthians which no local authority seemed able to control. The same holy Fortunatus, beloved disciple of St. Paul, who must be considered as perfectly familiar with Apostolic teachings and ordinances, passing by St. John the Evangelist, and all other dignitaries of Holy Church in the East, hastened to Rome to seek and demand from the Head of the Universal Church the Successor of St. Peter, the interposition of supreme authority to put a termination to the unhappy disturbance at Corinth. The Bishop of Rome addressed himself to the duty of instructing the distant Church, and the whole affair was conducted in so matter-of-fact, and in so official a manner...with so prudent yet firm exhibition of admitted plenitude of teaching and governing authority, that complete success was the immediate result. From the reading, alone, of the history of the transaction, the Supreme Headship of the Bishop of Rome shines out clearly----St. Clement sending four legates to act in his name, to the distant East, with instructions to exercise his authority and power, and to bring back to him, speedily, an account of all proceedings. Now, all this, under the very eyes, and within reach of the living voice of the Evangelist St. John, must be considered as demonstrating the fullest exercise of Papal official prerogatives, far back in the history of the Catholic Church, when, as yet, the clock of the Christian centuries had not struck--One. Papal pretensions at a very early date, to be sure! And, besides that, the Pope who exercised the pretensions was a bosom friend and beloved disciple of Sts. Peter and Paul, and had been consecrated at St. Peter's own hands to exercise the very pretensions which are related of him. Moreover, good Protestant friend, the name of that true Pope, Clement, predecessor of our Pius the Great, all the time he was indulging in the exercise of Papal prerogatives' was written and indelibly registered in the "Book of Life," as we are infallibly assured. *Philip.* iv. 3.

N. B.   Thus, dear reader, the Holy Catholic Church greets you in the field of authentic history at the close of the first Christian century.   St. Clement was Bishop of Rome and exercised supreme pastoral jurisdiction over the Eastern churches.   St. John, the Evangelist, was yet living.   St. Ignatius, consecrated by Sts. Peter and Paul, was Bishop of Antioch.   St. Polycarp, disciple and bosom friend of St. John the Evangelist, was Bishop of Smyrna,..."the Angel of the Church of Smyrna," most highly commended by Jesus Himself, and pronounced to be undeserving of slightest reproach. *Acts* ii, 8.   Hundreds of Apostolic men, learned and holy, who had received the faith, and the gifts of God, directly from the Apostles of Christ themselves, were living and testifying and propagating the true doctrines of the crucified Jesus everywhere.   These men *knew* the things whereof they testified; and, as we hope to be recognized as believers of the revelations of Jesus Christ, and followers of the teachings of His holy Apostles, we must accept and revere the testimony of these Apostolic men, the sounds of whose voices reach to our ears in most clearly authenticated manner and form.

It will not be denied, in the face of St. Paul, and in contradiction of the "Book of Life," that the Christian Church of Rome, Pope and all, was in all respects the pure and true Church of Jesus Christ at the close of the first Christian century.   Catholics! we are, thus early, in clear, undisputed possession,...to be assailed, always, to be dislodged, never!

XIX.

OUR HISTORICAL POSITIONS ARE IMPREGNABLE.

We consider that just here is the proper place to invite attention to the real and absolute value, in themselves of the varied historical monuments and other documentary records which we bring to bear upon the special topics treated in these pages. We do not argue our subject matter theologically, nor, properly speaking, do we discuss the great question in a controversial style. In our case, the call to the front, and the gage of battle thrown by assailing gainsayers, demand only an armed readiness in the open field of authentic and true history. Hence it is that, for present purposes we ask nothing, even for the sacred writings, except a recognition of the authority which all sane minds are obliged to yield to every "true and certain" narrative of facts.

Candid friend, have you ever pondered the magnificent grandeur, material and literary, of the "Augustan age?" One temporal master governed the universal, known, civilized, world. The boundaries of the vast Empire touched the Atlantic, the Danube, the Euphrates, the Severn, the Tyne, and the burning sands of the Sahara. Within the periphery of the boundary lines, all of Europe, Africa, and Asia, was...the Roman Empire. Rome, the City, was the Empire epitomized. Humanitarian civilization had reached the very acme of enjoyable splendor. Everywhere, the blazing sun of human learning was shining with most dazzling effulgence. So, you see it was no age of ignorance or mental darkness when our Holy Catholic Church was born into this world. It was no uncivilized place or time where and when the one Supreme Apostle of Christ fixed, permanently, the See which, forever, was to be the governing See of Christendom. It was not because Rome was great and powerful the See became premanent, but, the pre-eminent See was fixed at Rome because Rome was the capital city of the world. St.

Peter, doubless acted according to Christ's instructions. Most certainly the selection was both humanly wise and divinely prompted.

Rome, the capital city of the known world, for ages, by mysterious orderings of the Omnipotent, had been preparing for its sublime Christian destiny. It was a grand center-point of operations for the Vicar on earth of Jesus Christ from whom, and to whom, messengers of the Gospel were to go and come, from and to all parts of the known world. "Through Sixteen large gates the Romans had egress to the surrounding country. No less than eight hundred and twenty paved high roads led into the different provinces, forming with their intersections a net-work, beginning at the golden mile-stone erected by Augustus in the forum at the foot of the Capitol, as the central point of the Empire, and spreading thence over the whole known civilized world." It was a most befitting geographical spot, and there St. Peter established the "Apostolic Holy Roman See." Thus the Catholic Church and her Papacy became seated at Rome, by divine arrangement, whilst all the commissioned Apostles of Jesus Christ were yet living and laboring and planting Churches.

It was the will of God that Christianity, in its origin, should take position in the world without the aid of human learning in its original human founders, lest after ages might have a chance to say that it was cunningly introduced as a new philosophic system. It was the will of God that Christianity should become an established fact in the world unaided, unprotected, unrecognized, by Cæsar, lest, in after ages, men might have a pretext for saying that its early success was owing to the aid and comfort afforded by the temporal power, and lest it might be said that the Church of Rome became the chief because she was established in the first city of the empire, under the imperial sanction and favor. In addition to all this, it was the will of God, evident to all mankind, that learned philosophers, renowned statesmen and warriors, distinguished and wealthy magnates, and multitudes of less noted individuals, led to conviction by evidences of the truth of Christianity,--under influences of supernatural grace,--became at once most fervent and most faithful Christians. And, furthermore, dear reader, it was the plan of God that during three centuries St. Peter and his successors should manifestly exercise supreme spiritual sovereignty over the entire world, whilst relentless persecution raged, so that it is forever in evidence that civil influence never could nor can claim any share in the establishment or in the upholding of the supreme pontificate. For about three hundred years the poor old Popes, shut up in the catecombs which bordered the Roman roads, reigned over universal Christendom. From the habitations, rather of death than of life, their government was obeyed; men rendered them homage; their See was recognized as the source of all jurisdiction; the Bishop of Rome was saluted as the Prince of Pastors and the Bishop of Bishops; and, in testimony of all this, besides numberless historical admissions of earliest days, we have the records of numerous striking acts, by which men could never be deceived. Thus, with regard to the true origin of what heretics call "Papal pretensions," there have existed, from the beginning, absolutely indisputable proofs. The establishment of the Papacy at Rome, just as the Apostles were finally separating to subdue the world to Christ, and possessing as it did acknowledged plenitude of teaching and governing authority over the whole world—was the work of God. The continuance of the Papacy at Rome until now, possessing as it does acknowledged plenitude of teaching and governing authority over the whole world, is proof positive of the Divinity of Jesus Christ.

Can we satisfy the general reader that the historical evidences which we bring to bear upon the special topics treated of in these pages are absolutely undeniable? Most certainly we can! We produce such historical monuments and documentary records, only, against the genuineness and reliability of which, as to facts detailed, neither renegade Christian nor scoffing infidel has ever dared to whisper a doubt...though renegade and scoffer always try to evade their damning evidences by childish, or more silly than childish, explanations and comments.

Since the overthrow of the Roman Empire of the West, A. D. 476, vast libraries of the world have been destroyed, and numberless precious writings of early Christian ages have perished. There escaped, however, and still exist, a goodly number of early Christian literary monuments, furnishing to us, at first hands, all needed illuminating evidences concerning earliest Christian belief and practices. We beg to mention a few of the works to which we may have occasion to refer. All said works referred to are undeniably authentic and historically reliable...are admitted to be so by Christian and infidel...are revered as such by Catholic and Protestant. We have *Two Epistles to the Corinthians* from the pen of that St. Clement whose name was in the book of life, *Philip.* iv, 3, who was a contemporary of the Apostles, and who was, moreover, fourth Bishop of Rome. These *Epistles* used to be read during the celebration of the divine mysteries, after the inspired writings, in Churches of the East, as authoritative instructions from the supreme teaching Head of the universal Christian Church. *Eusebius, Ch. Hist.*, b. iv, c. 23.

Next, we have the *Seven Epistles* to various Churches of St. Ignatius, Bishop of Antioch, a contemporary of the Apostles, and, like St. Clement, consecrated Bishop by them. Both Clement and Ignatius were, for nearly forty years, on most familiar terms of intercourse with St. John the Evangelist, death not intervening to break the tie of intimacy until about the last year of the first Christian century. We have the writings of St. Justin Martyr, one of the most learned of heathen philosophers, who became a Christian A. D. 137, and who, at Rome, in order to repel calumnies charged upon the Christians, explained in writing to the Roman Emperor and Senate the true doctrines and mode of worship of the Catholic Church of that day. Tertullian, a prodigy of learning, became a Christian and wrote many works which are in our possession. He is an excellent witness of the faith and the facts of his day, though in his latter years pride and a wounded morose temper led him to the expression of personal *opinions* heretical in themselves and at variance with all Christian faith and facts of preceding times, as he himself had demonstrated. Tertullian was born A. D. 160 and died A. D. 245.

St. Irenæus, born A. D. 120, died A. D. 202, was educated at the feet of St. Polycarp, the Angel of the Church of Smyrna, commended by Jesus Christ Himself, *Apoc.* or *Revel.* ii. 8. Polycarp had been the favorite disciple of St. John the Evangelist, and must be admitted as a true witness and faithful expounder of the faith and practices of the early faithful. St. Irenæus,

Bishop of Lyons in Gaul, filled with Christian knowledge from the lips of St. John the Evangelist through Polycarp, wrote five books against heresies, which books are extant, and are clearly demonstrative of numerous details of the ancient Catholic Christian Faith and the ancient practical duties of Christian life. St. Hegesippus, a holy and learned man, a convert to Christianity, and a Catholic Priest of Jerusalem, wrote a *History of the Church* in five books, a narration of events from the date of our Lord's crucifixion until A. D. 170. The writer visited all the principal Churches of Christendom that he might narrate nothing but what he knew to be true and certain from his own personal investigation. He arrived in Rome A. D. 160, in the time of Pope Anicetus, and remained there until A. D. 177, when Pope Eleutherius governed the Universal Church. Having completed his *Church History* during his sojourn at the Head See of Christendom, Hegesippus returned to Jerusalem, where he died A. D 180. The five books of our oldest ecclesiastical historian have perished, but the great Eusebius has preserved many interesting quotations from them.

Eusebius had been imprisoned for the faith A. D 309. He was chosen Archbishop of Cæsarea in Palestine A. D. 314. He wrote many works, and was a most thorough scholar. We shall mention only his ten books of *Ecclesiastical History*, bringing down a methodical narration of Christian affairs from the beginning until the defeat of Licinius, A. D. 323, when Constantine, the first Christian Emperor, first became sole temporal master of the entire Roman Empire. Scholars agree that Eusebius was one of the most learned prelates of antiquity, and a man of universal reading, but not much given to polishing-up his pen-productions, which is a common fault of those who make learning and knowledge their chief business. Eusebius is a faithful narrator and witness of all events preceding A. D. 323. Theodoret, a man of extraordinary learning and piety, became Bishop of Cyrus, eighty miles from Antioch, A. D. 423. His valuable works are many. He wrote *Church History* in five books, commencing where Eusebius left off, A. D. 323, and brought the narrative of Christian affairs down to A. D. 429. The celebrated Greek historians Sozomen and Socrates furnish to us a knowledge of facts down to about A. D. 451. That giant of learning, St. Jerome, born A. D. 327, died A. D. 420, among other productions, compiled a most useful work entitled *A Catalogue of Illustrious Men*, being one hundred and thirty-five chapters treating of Ecclesiastical Writers of preceding ages.

Want of time and limited space forbid us to particularize decades of prized existing folios from the pens of such men as Cyprian of Carthage, Athanasius of Alexandria, the Cyrils of Alexandria and Jerusalem, Chrysostom of Constantinople, Gregory of Nazianzen and his namesake of Nyssa, Ambrose of Milan, Augustine of Hippo Regius, and others whose works are most profoundly learned and most conspicuously genuine, and upon whose truth-telling pages we may cast our eyes whenever we so desire. Our purpose requires us to refer only to writers who flourished before the overthrow of the Western Roman Empire, and against whose productions the finger of hesitancy as to absolute credibility cannot be pointed. The number might be doubled and trebled but we have mentioned more than a sufficiency.

When the above luminaries penned their productions the writers had the precious privilege of thousands of original manuscripts of which not even the names have come down to our day. Humanly speaking it was a glorious epoch of human learning and mental greatness when the Catholic Church made willing captives to the faith of Christ nearly every one considered worth the naming in those ages of literary splendor.

Our reason for calling attention to the above enumerated ancient authorities is that the general reader may know and appreciate the character of each witness, when one may be called upon to give testimony, and that, after perusing our evidences, every reader may be capable and prepared to bring in an intelligent verdict of " *Willful lying in the first degree* " against Martin Luther, Ignatz Von Dœllinger, and Hyacinth Loyson,--representative men...true specimen samples of all those who have dogmatized the contrary of that which they knew in their souls to be the truth about Papal Supremacy, which Supremacy, it is easily seen, always involved and included that other much calumniated prerogative, Papal Infallibility.• This "Old Catholic" can never realize any practical distinction between Papal Supremacy and Papal Infallibility. Dear reader, turn to pages 14, 15, and to pages 19, 20, ponder the propositions as they are numbered on said pages, and form an idea, if you can, of any practical difference between a Pope Supreme and a Pope Infallible.

Martin Luther's thirteenth proposition, opposed by Eck, was as follows: "That the Roman Church is superior to all others is proved from the forged decrees of Roman Pontiffs who have lived within the last four hundred years; against which are the authentic records of eleven hundred years; the words of Scripture; and the decrees of the Council of Nice, the most sacred of all the councils." That is to say, Martin Luther pledges his reputation for veracity, that the supremacy of the

Roman Pontiff was never heard of in the Christian Church until after A. D. 1100. Ignatz Von Dœllinger proclaims to the world that "Analytical Treatment of History" demonstrates facts which flatly contradict the defined dogma of Papal Infallibility. Hyacinth Loyson writes a letter to the *New York Independent*, saying that he must "remain constant to the immovable faith of the Catholic Church, and the *primitive* faith of the Church of Rome;" but he refuses "adherence to the pretended dogma, *new* and *heretical*, of Papal Infallibility."

We shall not allude to causes or motives. Suffice it to say that these men have impugned the known truth, and they, needs, were obliged to pretend some grounds for their novelties of doctrine. Luther speaks of *frigid* decrees since A. D. 1100; Dœllinger and Co., with some modern Protestants, boldly hint at forged documents of an earlier period, by which documents alone, they assert, modern Papal pretensions are proved and sustained. At the risk of a sound chiding for prolixity, we must say something about the so-called forged documents. The reader will please cultivate a little patience; the contents of this section, though, perhaps, tedious reading, will serve very much to a comprehension of the chief subject matter of our pages.

The *official* decrees of the Popes before A. D. 384 have perished, but we have abundance of other ecclesiastical documents, as this section proves, which enlighten us about the events of the first three centuries of the Papacy. Authentic *official* decretals of the Popes since A. D. 384 are not wanting. In the days of Charlemagne, about A. D. 800, a "collection of canons" was scattered through the West, brought from Spain by one Isidore surnamed *Mercator* or the *Merchant*. The decretals from St. Clement, A. D. 100, to St. Sericius,

A. D. 384, did not emanate from those whose names they bear. "They are made up of long passages from the Fathers" who lived long after, as St. Leo the Great, A. D. 461: St. Gregory the Great, A. D. 604, and others. These *forged* decretals were made up of the very sentences and expressions of the laws, of the ancient canons, and of the Holy Fathers who flourished A. D. 100 to A. D. 700. The matters of which they treat do not belong to the period to which they are ascribed. The dates are false, that is all.

Wherefore the pother? The Isidorian collection of canons is not, never was, considered as a basis of authority in the Catholic Church, for the purpose of defending "Papal pretensions." Opponents of the Papacy seem to "go for" the ancient citadel of Roman Supremacy as if Mercator's compilation were its only grand fortified position of defence, whereas, good gracious! the poor anti-papists only make a show of themselves to the world "playing Chinese antics before an old mound which was never used for military purposes, and which nobody ever dreamed of defending." The amiable and learned convert, James Kent Stone, has very accurately expressed the whole Catholic idea about the harp of one string-- the Isidorian compilation--the only historical instrument upon which "new departures" from Catholicity ever pretend to strike up a tune against the venerable antiquity of Papal Supremacy. They do not seem to have mental acumen sufficient to discover that all the importance of Isidore's decretals grows out of the pre-existing admitted Supremacy, not the Supremacy from the ante-dated imposture.

CHAPTER SEVENTH.

XX.

ROMAN SUPREMACY AN ADMITTED PUBLIC FACT FROM EARLIEST DAYS OF CHRISTIANITY.

The Evangelists demonstrate to us, as we have seen, Simon Peter bearing a special commission under the seal of the Great King. St. Luke, Acts xv, exhibits to us the Bishop of Rome, in person, presiding over the great Apostolic Council of Jerusalem. St. Paul's opinion of, and beseeching admonition to, the Holy Roman Church, long before his first visit thereto, are of divinely inspired record. *Rom.* i, 8, xvi, 17. The "Epistles to the Corinthians" of St. Clement, fourth Bishop of Rome, that Pope's acts of supremacy, and the character of the Holy Father himself, *Phil* iv, 3. have been considered. No man can have any claim, at all, to the name Christian who does not confess that the Christian Church of Rome, with Pope Clement as her Bishop, possessed the pure faith of Christ, and taught the same with infallible certainty A. D. 42----100, to the end of the first Christian century. Since that date, when did that Church cease to possess the same precise faith, or to teach it with the same infallible certainty? *When?* Aye, that's the question!

St. Ignatius Martyr had been consecrated Bishop of Antioch by Sts. Peter and Paul. Like Pope St. Clement he was for about forty years a contemporary and an intimate friend of St. John the Evangelist. Condemned by the Emperor Trajan to be devoured by wild beasts at Rome, Ignatius set out under a guard of soldiers for the imperial city. On the way he wrote seven epistles to so many Churches. The epistles to six of the Churches were filled with instructions, exhortations, and admonitions regarding faith and duties, and were addressed: "To the Church which is at Ephesus," "To the Church which is at Philadelphia," etc. The Epistle to the Roman Church is of different style. The aged companion of the Apostles begs that the Roman Christians will not interfere to hinder his obtaining the crown of martyrdom. The true faith, the pure worship, and the great virtues which characterized the Holy Catholic Church of Rome are touched upon with peculiar earnestness. The particular address of that one epistle is very remarkable and significant: "To the beloved Church which is enlightened, which PRESIDES in the country of the Romans, worthy of God, fitly regulated and governed, PRESIDING in charity, etc." St. Ignatius seems to have thought of the Roman Church as did St. Paul. The testimony of that early Apostolic Bishop of Antioch, first dignitary and most aged prelate of the East, about the "beloved, enlightened, fitly regulated and governed Church which PRESIDES in the country of the Romans," is very plain and very specific. The Anglican universities would rather that Ignatius had not penned those words. But, there they are!

A. D. 158 St. Anicetus was Bishop of Rome. The "Angel of the Church of Smyrna," St. Polycarp, disciple of St. John the Evangelist, commended by Jesus Christ Himself, *Apoc.* or *Revel.* ii, 8, being very old, undertook a journey to Rome on official business, to solicit on his own behalf, and on behalf of other Eastern Bishops, the forbearance of the Roman Pontiff about a *disciplinary* difference which existed between the Church

11

of Rome and the Eastern Churches regarding the time of celebrating the festival of Easter. Anicetus honored Polycarp by inviting him to celebrate the holy mysteries at the Pope's own altar, and Polycarp returned to the East to report that Holy Anicetus, Bishop of Rome, had conceded to the Orientals the solicited privilege of continuing to celebrate Easter as had been their custom. We have the facts from *St. Irenæus*, b. iii, c. 3, *Eusebius*, b. v, c. 24, *Jerome, Catal. Illust. Men*, c. 17. Some years afterward certain sowers of dissension began to dogmatize that the Asiatic disciplinary custom of celebrating Easter on the "fourteenth day" was a divine obligation----an open heresy which would inculcate the obligation of Christians to observe the Jewish ceremonial law. Hence it was that, to guard purity of faith, subsequent Popes insisted upon uniformity of discipline everywhere regarding this point—and insisted with so much tenacity of purpose and so much manifestation of universal jurisdiction.

St. Hegesippus, our oldest ecclesiastical historian, came to Rome A. D. 160, two years after St. Polycarp had been there, and under the same Pope Anicetus. He had visited all the principal Churches East and West, that he might write his history from personal knowledge. He remained twenty-seven years in Rome, completing his history in five book, from the crucifixion to A. D. 179. Hear his testimony :---" Though certain men have disturbed the Church by broaching heresies, yet down to this time--A. D. 170--no Episcopal See or particular Church has fallen into error ; in all places they have preserved inviolably the truths delivered by Christ." *Euseb.* b. iv, c. 22.

St. Irenæus was the beloved disciple of St. Polycarp. For many years Irenæus was accustomed to listen to the things which John the Evangelist had committed to Polycarp, and which Polycarp was careful to commit to other faithful men able to teach others also. *Tim.* ii, 2. We may almost call St. Irenæus an immediate faithful disciple of our Lord's beloved Apostle John. He was deputed by the faithful of Lyons, A. D. 177, to visit Rome and to consult Pope Eleutherius on some ecclesiastical matters, and on his return he was made Bishop of Lyons, where he suffered martyrdom A. D. 202. St. Irenæus must be admitted as a thoroughly informed and competent witness of Christian affairs in his day. He wrote five books against heresies. He speaks of the Roman Church and gives a list of the Bishops of Rome from St. Peter to St. Eleutherius, styling Eleutherius the twelfth after St. Peter. He tells us that "the Apostles certainly delivered the truth and all the mysteries of our faith to their successors the pastors; to these, therefore, we ought to have recourse to learn them, especially to the greatest Church, the most ancient and known to all, founded at Rome by the two most glorious Apostles Peter and Paul, for with this Church (of Rome) on account of her Superior Headship---*propter potentiorem principalitatem*---it is necessary that every Church---that is the faithful everywhere----should agree, in which the Apostolic tradition has been always preserved by those who are on all sides." *St. Irenæus*, b. iii, c. 3. It will be borne in mind that Irenæus speaks from the fullness of his Apostolic teaching, and his utterances must be taken as the accepted faith of Christendom in his day. Now, it is not easy to conceive how every Church, and the faithful everywhere, could be bound by divine precept to agree in faith with the Church of Rome on account of the Superior Headship of that Church, unless that Church *was* the Superior Head of all other Churches, and unless that Church of Rome was divinely protected from possibility of leading the other Churches or the faithful into error. Infallibility of the Roman Pontiff shines out conspicuously from the testimony of Irenæus. In fact, EVERY PROOF OF THE SUPREMACY IMPLIES THE INFALLIBILITY.

Stern old Tertullian, the first in time of the Latin Fathers, was a convert and a priest of Carthage. He was born about A. D. 160, and, if we may so express it, was a man loaded down with sacred and profane learning. About A. D. 200 his severity of temperament caused him to be deceived by the hypocritical rigidity of certain heretics of the day, and he fell into a little unpleasantness with the Bishop of Rome and comported himself rather rebelliously in language. We do not question Tertullian, however, about his opinion or this or that speculative point of doctrine, our present object is to take his deposition as to the status in the world in his day of the Bishop of Rome. We question him concerning an existing, publicly, universally, known fact of his time. He may be considered as a reluctant witness of the Supremacy of the Roman Pontiff, but the reluctance makes his testimony the more decided. The Pope had issued a decree against Tertullian's favorites. The decree is thus noticed: "I hear that an edict has been published, and, indeed, a peremptory one, namely, the Sovereign Pontiff, THE BISHOP OF BISHOPS, proclaims, etc." (*Tertull.* Book to Praxeas.) One of the most learned of latter day Protestants, the Prince of modern Anti-Romanists, George Stanley Faber, in his *Difficulties of Romanism*, Note, page 261, edit. Phil., discourses thus:— "In the time of Tertullian a considerable advance had plainly been made by the See of Rome, in the claim of the Primacy, inasmuch as he calls the Bishop of that

Church the Supreme Pontiff, and distinguished him with the title of Bishop of Bishops." Yes, indeed, Friend Faber, and gainsayers all; a considerable advance!

St. Victor was Bishop of Rome A. D. 192--202. Certain disturbers began to dogmatize that the observance of the "fourteenth day" was a duty of divine obligation. Victor condemned the heresy, and desired to have the discipline of the whole Church uniform in the celebration of the Easter festivity, that imminent danger to the true faith might be more thoroughly averted. From the catacombs the word went fotrh over the world, and we read of Councils everywhere assembling *to accept the instructions* OF ROME and to promulgate the accepted instructions. Some Asiatics demurred and put in a plea that Pope Anicetus had sanctioned adherence to the old discipline which had prevailed among them from earliest times. Polycrates of Ephesus was disobedient and obstinate--Victor threatened to excommunicate the recusants.

St. Irenæus and other holy Bishops entreated Victor to forbear for a time, as the matter was only one of discipline; and so the matter rested for the time being. The affair affords one of the most splendid evidences of the universal admission of the Supremacy of the Bishop of Rome over the whole of Christendom. The persistent exercise of the Supremacy in all its plenitude by Victor is proof that there was full consciousness among all concerned that it had a rightful existence. Some were disobedient, and as a palliative of their undutiful behavior, they alleged the authority of a preceding Pope, Anicetus, who had allowed what Victor would prohibit. The stubborn few did not advert to the serious motives which prompted the severe solicitude of Victor, which motives had no existence in the circumstances attending the visit of Polycarp to Anicetus. The disobedience of Bishop Polycrates and other Asiatics did no violence to holy faith, so, at the urgent solicitation of many holy Bishops from various parts of the world, for the sake of peace, Victor permitted the Asiatic custom to prevail for a further time, until, finally, the discipline of the Roman Church prevailed everywhere. Now, who is senseless enough to believe that, at a time when Bishops were numerous, and learned and independent, and whilst the Bishop of Rome was hiding in the catacombs, and whilst, thence, Victor was manifesting great determination to enforce obedience by the exercise of extreme coercive spiritual authority, and whilst the high-tempered, independent Bishops were not in the most amiable of moods, no one ever penned a word or uttered a whisper charging the Bishop of Rome with pretensions to an authority which was not acknowledged? Why was that? Ah, indeed! echo answers—why?

Councils of Africa, with great and learned prelates presiding, put forth decrees that baptism administered by heretics, even when proper matter and form were observed, was invalid and should be renewed. St. Stephen, Bishop of Rome, A. D. 253--257, saw danger threatening the unity of faith, and he defined the true faith and decreed that "no innovation is to be allowed, but the tradition of the Church derived from the Apostles is to be inviolably maintained." The promise of Infallibility not having been made to individual Bishops, nor to any majority or minority of Bishops assembled in council or dispersed, some were not pleased with the definition proclaimed by Stephen, but no one of the great and learned and independent minds of that age thought of calling in question the authority of St. Stephen, of the Roman See, to take cognizance of the African decisions and to pronounce "finally" upon them. The Africans allowed themselves to fancy that the Bishop of Rome had been wrongly informed about facts in the case, and so, certain eminent ones manifested some warm obstinacy against the Papal decree. The Bishop of Rome menaced the recusants with excommunication—threatened to *mark them*, as St. Paul had enjoined, *Rom.* xvi, 17, if they persisted in obstinate disobedience. After that, "all the multitude held their peace!" And after the multitude held their peace, the Bishops all over the world, each in his own See, like St. James at Jerusalem, rose up and said to his own flock, "Men, brethren, hearken to me; this is what Stephen said, etc." *Acts* xv.

St. Dyonisius was Bishop of Rome A. D 259--269. St. Dyonisius the greatest ecclesiastical dignitary of the East, Archbishop of Alexandria, was accused to the Bishop of Rome of holding and teaching erroneous doctrines concerning the Holy Trinity. The Roman Pontiff cited the Alexandrian Prelate to give an account of his faith. He of Alexandria most nobly responded to the citation of the Roman Sovereign Pontiff, and proved very clearly that he agreed in faith with the Roman standard.

It was a period of fiercest persecution. There were Bishops by hundreds throughout the Empire. The ferocious Emperor Decius, A. D. 249--251, took but little more notice of Bishops than he did of the rest of the faithful, but he knew of One Bishop whose authority among Christians was so conspicuous--and so supereminent over all other Bishops---that his imperial rage became so furious as to draw from him a declaration of willingness to tolerate a rival to his imperial sceptre rather than permit the existence of a Bishop of Rome.

Dear reader, can you guess why Decius regarded the Roman Pontiff from a different standpoint than he did the numberless other Bishops of his Empire? The pagans knew the eminent dignity of that "Bishop of Bishops!"

A. D. 168, Paul of Samosata, Bishop of Antioch, had been deposed for heresy, but was protected by Zenobia, Queen of Palmyra. Aurelian's army defeated the Queen's troops and took possession of the city. The deposed Bishop held possession of the Episcopal mansion. Appeal was made to the Emperor to dispossess the heretical incumbent. What did Aurelian know about who was orthodox or who was heretical? Nothing. But he knew the plan of organization and the mode of conducting business affairs among the Christians. The imperial decision was:—"Let the property be confirmed to him to whom the Bishop of Rome and his Italian Bishops shall adjudge it." Heathens as well as Christians knew, in those days, that the Bishop of Rome was the "tribunal of last resort from which there could be no appeal," and the tribunal to which, from the days of St. Peter, all major causes were brought up and determined without further hope of reconsideration forever.

A RETROSPECT OF THE SITUATION.

XXI.

Dearly Beloved Protesting Friend!—Our "Analytical Treatment of History" has been brought down to the commencement of the fourth century of the Christian era. Your humble servant, "An Old Catholic," begs to whisper a few sensible words in your ear. "Stand thou here with me" and let us take a brief, but cool and unbiassed, retrospect of the situation. The time is

A. D. 314, Jan. 31. St. Sylvester, the thirty-third Bishop
of Rome, has just succeeded to supreme headship of
the Catholic Church. Until now the succession to the
Roman Pontificate was a succession to martyrdom, and
the prefix, "Saint," by universal admission of all Christian ages and nations, rightfully precedes the name of
every one of Sylvester's predecessors in the Roman See.

To every believer in the revelations of Holy Bible it
is in evidence that from Adam to Noah, from Noah to
Abraham, from Abraham to Moses, from Moses to Jesus
Christ, God never left himself without an Infallible
human teacher and witness of His Divine revelation to
man. It is in evidence that Jesus Christ organized on
earth a *most perfect* Church of God, to continue in unity
of faith and indefectibility of doctrine until the end of
the world. It is in evidence, if we are to believe St.
Paul, St. Clement, St. Fortunatus, St. Ignatius, St. Polycarp, St. Irenæus, St. Hegesippus, and other immediate
successors of the Apostles, that the Church of Rome, in
their days, "preserved inviolably the truths delivered
by Jesus Christ,"----and that the Church of Rome was
the "PRESIDING CHURCH"----with which, on account of
its "Superior Apostolic Headship," it was necessary
that all other churches should agree. It is thus that the
facts of true history make plainly known to every candid
mind the Catholic "situation" at Rome during the period of time from our Lord's crucifixion until A. D. 202.

What do you think of the character and competency
of the witnesses? What is your judgment about their
original sources of information? How do you like the
straight-forward plainness of their depositions regarding
the "Roman question" in those early days?

Coming down further in the centuries, dear friend, there stand before you, in the line of witnesses, Eusebius, Jerome, and Augustine; there are the Cyrils and the Gregories ; and there you may observe Athanasius, Basil, Chrysostom, and Ambrose; and others, too, a goodly number, whose names will readily suggest themselves to the historical student, holy prodigies of learning and sanctity, whose reputation has ever been, and is now, held in the most exalted esteem by every scholar in Christendom. All of them flourished before the overthrow of the Western Roman Empire, and all of them, to a man, depose and say that down to their days the Christian Church at Rome, under the "Holy Bishops of the Apostolic Roman See," was divinely invested with, and duly exercised, plenitude of teaching and governing authority, which *universal* authority was *universally* recognized as pertaining to St. Peter's See.

The first century of our era, A. D. 29--100, from our Lord's Ascension until the death of the Evangelist St. John, is known as the Apostolic age. The second and third centuries, and until A. D. 312, we call the iron age of heathen persecution. The fourth and a portion of the fifth centuries, from Constantine the Great until the destruction of the Roman Empire in the West, historians designate as the "Golden Age of Christianity." With regard to the "Roman question," considered merely as a fact of history, this writer, already, has placed before his readers very plain evidences that, in the Apostolic age, all Christendom, *numerically* assembled in an upper chamber of Jerusalem, *Acts* i, recognized St. Peter as the directing Head of the new organization. He has, also, called attention to a very striking fact which no Christian can ignore, namely, that all

Christendom, *representatively* assembled at Jerusalem,
Acts xv, recognized St. Peter, then Bishop of Rome, as
the directing and teaching Head, at the sound of whose
defining voice disputes ceased at once. Peter rose up
and spoke, and "they all held their peace." The Apostles, James the Less, John the Evangelist, and Paul,
were there. *They* deemed it no derogation to *their* noble
intellects to recognize and heed the directing authority
which Jesus Christ, their God and ours, had constituted
on earth and commanded all men to recognize and heed.
This "Old Catholic" considers their evidence, and their
example, as very damaging before a jury of honest-
minded Christians in the case of Outraged History *versus*
the great Luther, the great Dœllinger, and the little Hyacinth Loyson, impugners of the *known* truth. Against
the *known* lies of these men history points to the act,
also, of holy Fortunatus, disciple of St. Paul, going up to
St. Clement, and to the acts of Clement after Peter had
been dead about thirty years, and whilst John the Evangelist was yet living.

Dear Protesting friend, we, together, have interro-
gated men of the iron age, and you know what manner
of men were the witnesses---Ignatius, Polycarp, Irenæus,
and others, and you know what *they* said about that fact
of history which the indicted trio, (applauded with so
much display of ignorance by newspaperdom,) swear
upon their veracity to be no fact of history at all, but
only a novelty which ambition of the Roman Bishop
began to introduce cunningly by frigid decrees about
A. D. 1100,---a novelty which the Catholic Church always opposed with bold front, until, as Dœllinger and
Loyson say, July 18, 1871, when the Vatican Council,

under compulsion, (God bless us!) accepted a *new* article of faith from the dictation of Pius IX.

We might fill page after page with quotations from the great men of learning and sanctity who flourished during the "golden age of Christianity," but relative to "the Roman question," only one vein of thought, and one manner of expressing that thought, pervaded the whole literature of that age. Rome was on all hands acknowledged to be the incorrupt and incorruptible guardian of the faith of the fathers. Those who drank of her pure fountain were qualified for spreading revealed truth in its integrity throughout those regions in which human error had before prevailed. The Roman Bishop was recognized as supreme judge of all other Bishops in those things which pertained to God, according to the type Moses among the Children of Israel. The authority of the Holy Roman See, "the tribunal of last resort from which there could be no appeal," was always invoked in all the controversies and dissensions which arose among Christians during the whole period of time which we are now considering, namely, the first five centuries of the Christian era. The authority of the Holy Roman See was constantly invoked, and always manifested, from hiding-place of the catacombs no less than from the more splendid Basilica of later years. No fact of history was ever more clearly impressed upon the world's records. The greatest of all Protestant controversialists, the incomparable Leibnitz, tells us in his *Systema Theologicum* as follows: "The ancients unanimously attest that the Apostle Peter governed the Church, suffered martyrdom, and appointed his successor, in the City of Rome, the capital of the world; and, as by the divine law itself one of the Apostles, and the successor of this one among the bishops, was invested with pre-eminent power, in order that by him, as the visible centre of unity, the body of the Church might be bound together, and as no other bishop has ever been recognized under this relation, we justly acknowledge the Bishop of Rome to be chief of all the rest." In the domain of universal human knowledge, in modern times, there does not appear the name of a greater scholar than Leibnitz who lived and died an unbigotted Protestant.

Who can call in question the vast erudition, and the accuracy as to facts, of that apostate Catholic, Protestant infidel, Gibbon, in his brilliant History of the Decline and Fall of the Roman Empire and other writings? We understand appreciate and despise his sarcastic sneers and comments, but no man can set aside his narrated facts. Listen to Gibbon, *Memoir*, vol. i, c. 1: "A well informed man cannot resist the weight of evidence which establishes that in the whole period of the four first ages of the Church the principal points of the papistical doctrines were already admitted in theory and in practice."

George Stanley Faber, already quoted p. 84, admits Popery in full blast at Rome before A. D. 200, whilst Irenæus and such kind of men, who had received knowledge from Apostolic lips, were looking on and declaring the system to be the ordinance of Jesus Christ.

Hallam, that profound scholar of Anglicanism, does not like to have early Christian facts staring him too closely in the face, yet his self-respect as a writer of history compels him to give *the lie direct* to Luther & Co. on the Roman question in his *Middle Ages*, c. vii, p. 270,

Americ. edit. Says Hallam, who does not dare to be silent in the face of facts, but who hates to speak out boldly to the detriment of his cause, "Irenæus rather vaguely and Cyprian more positively admit, or rather assert, the Primacy of the Church of Rome, which the latter seems to have regarded as a kind of centre of Catholic unity."

☞ Kind reader, learned men of Christendom, in past and present ages, of all creeds and nations, agree with Faber, Gibbon, Leibnitz and Hallam, as to facts of history bearing upon our question. Their comments and private opinions are no concern of ours, nor do they affect the case. We shall trouble you with no further *individual* testimonies. Witnesses of the first standing, possessing *direct* knowledge of the facts whereof they testify, have given their depositions plainly and to the point. There can be no conceivable advantage derived from further quotations from particular writers of the early ages. Let us question Christendom henceforward, not individually, but as we may find it assembled in convention of the whole, or in Ecumenical Council.

☞ Hereafter, if desirable, "An Old Catholic" may have something to say to the good people of Perry County regarding the Roman Pontiff in his past and present relations to Cæsar and temporals. In the present chapters his unfoldings refer only to Papal universal Supremacy in spirituals, by divine right, and to *official* Papal Infallibility in all doctrinal matters, as a divinely instituted and historically demonstrated personal prerogative of the Bishop of Rome. In a few following pages the author will exhibit the East and the West—universal Christendom—century after century, boldly re-recognizing and fearlessly confessing Papal Supremacy and Papal Infallibility as God-established facts. Finally, he will disclose, historically, to the astonishment of some readers, *universal* Protestantism in the thirteenth year of its age, openly recognizing and fully anxious, *sub conditione*, to accept the entire "Catholic Situation," A. D. 1530.

CHAPTER EIGHTH.

XXII.

CONCILIAR EVIDENCES.—FIRST ECUMENICAL COUNCIL.

We are about to submit to our patient readers conciliar evidences regarding the Holy Roman Church and its Bishop, after God permitted more unrestrained freedom of action, outside the catacombs. In every well supplied library may be found the "Collections of Councils" by *Labbe*, by *Mansi*, by *Harduin;* principal works on that specific subject. Who would consult the large works may do so by application to the Very Rev. Superior of St. Joseph's College. He will take pleasure to introduce any enquirer for truth to the original testimonies of numberless giant intellects whom in vastness of knowledge the present generations of men *may* admire, but may never hope to emulate. To the general reader we earnestly recommend our English translation of "Darras' Church History" as a store-house of facts more specifically detailed than we can find room for in our little book.

A. D. 325, St. Sylvester was Bishop of Rome. Constantine the Great was temporal master of the whole known civilized world. It was deemed expedient that a general council should be held. With the consent of St. Sylvester, Bishop of Rome, a council of three hundred and twenty-five Bishops convened at Nice, in Bythinia, June 25, A. D. 325, and continued its sessions for five weeks. Osius, Bishop of Cordova, Spain, Vitus and Vincent, priests of Rome, in the name and by authority of St. Sylvester, presided over that dignified assembly. The legates, first of all, signed the decrees, and then the Bishops, according to rank, affixed their names. At the close of the council "A Synodical Letter" was prepared and signed by all the prelates, and was addressed to St. Sylvester, requesting "the blessed Roman Pontiff to confirm the decrees by his Apostolical authority." St. Sylvester confirmed the decrees. After the confirmation was promulgated, then, and not until then, the decrees were accepted and obeyed by the Universal Church. "Analytical Treatment of History" gives us this plain acknowledgment of conciliar powerlessness where the Roman Pontiff does not add the confirmation of Infallible Peter.

A. D. 347 Julius I. was Bishop of Rome. What is called an "Appendix to the council of Nice" was held at Sardica, a town of Illyricum. There were assembled more than three hundred Bishops, presided over by Archidamas and Philoxenes, merely Priests, and Leo, only a Deacon, legates of the Holy Bishop of Rome. No decrees of faith were submitted for action, disciplinary affairs only, passed over by the assembly at Nice, engaged attention at Sardica. Proceedings were *certified up* to Rome, as usual, with an humble request for confirmation by Apostolical authority of the Holy See. This council of Sardica has always enjoyed the same consideration in the Church, as to authority, which a general council enjoys, because all the conditions were present. It pleased God that this council did enact twenty-one canons of discipline, the third, fourth and seventh of which record a *public recognition* of an inalienable right or privilege possessed by every Bishop, in fact a right belonging to every one of the faithful—the right of appeal to the Bishop of Rome. There was no conferring of a right, but only a recognition of the existence of a right, for the Bishop of Rome was the "Head of all the Bishops," and he was from the beginning the "court of last resort" to whom, upon the arising of disputing or dissension, every one had a right to go to seek for justice and truth. The occasion of the recognition was this: certain good Bishops had been harshly treated by some Synods in the East and had appealed to Rome. The Pope examined the cases, and sent the Bishops back, each to his own See. The Synodical Bishops of the East who had deposed the appellant Bishops received the returned prelates with every token of respectful deference to the Supreme authority of the Roman Pontiff, and this assembly of Sardica gives to the world recorded evidence that the Bishop of Rome, independently of acts of councils, possessed authority of setting aside all judgments of courts below. It was a splendid confession of faith of an Ecumenical Council (Appendix of Nice) that the Pope was somebody; even before the frigid decrees after A. D. 1100.

The two great historians of the period refer to the circumstances in very plain words: "The Bishop of Rome, because the care of all belonged to him by the dignity of his See, restored every one to his church. *Sozomen*, b. iii, c. 7. "Julius, by virtue of the prerogatives of his See, sent the Bishops into the East, restoring to each one his See." *Socrates*, b. ii, c. 15.

Meeting with facts like these, the great luminary of modern British literature, Henry Hallam, *Middle Ages*, c. vii, p. 270 writes;—"the opinion of the Roman See's superiority seems to have prevailed very much in the fourth century. Fleury brings remarkable proofs of this from Socrates, Sozomen, Ammianus Marcellinus, and Optatus. · "Other learned Protestants, who wish to keep up a respectable appearance of consistency in their historical remarks about those early times, but who, for the sake of their cause, dare not look the facts in the face, never fail to "slur the notes " most unmelodously by the cool remark:——"It does seem that the Bishop of Rome began to acquire an ascendency over all other Bishops at a very early date!"

Poor fellows! well, it does seem so indeed! It does seem, from "Analytical Treatment of History," that the Bishop of Rome began to acquire an ascendency over the other Bishops at a very early date! Well, it does! Ask James, and John, and Paul, and Barnabas, and Clement, and Ignatius, and Polycarp, and Irenæus, and Tertullian, and the inimical Emperors Decius and Aurelian, and all the great lights of the subsequent "Golden age of Christianity." It does, indeed, seem that Papal pretensions began at a very early date!

All the chiefs of Protestantism, in Germany, ecclesiastics and laics, headed by Luther, Melancthon, and the others, A. D. 1530, in their confession of faith called the *Confession of Augsburg*, professed the obligation of all men to receive and obey the first six Ecumenical Councils of Christendom. Thus, their registered sworn declaration is on file, and is here offered in evidence that Protestantism embodied, did, A. D. 1530, recognize the Church of Rome and its Bishops as being ALL RIGHT down to A. D. 680. If the worthy chiefs of the reformation were inspired of God when they proposed adhesion to the first six Ecumenical Councils, it is a splendid testimony in favor of Rome and the Pope; if they were not inspired of God, but were prompted, *Aliunde*, as Cicero would say, then we can. understand how, why, and wherefore, Luther, in the morning, used to swear *by* the Pope of Rome, and with his boon companions, in the evening, in the public room of the "Black Eagle" tavern, Wittemberg, used to swear *at* both Rome and the Pope.

The Establishment which the British Parliament set up in their "Island Home" in place of the Church of Jesus Christ is bound, by order of Queen Elizabeth, to accept and abide by the acts and decrees of the first four Ecumenical Councils. See *Confession of Augsburg*, and also, xxxix Artic. Ch. Eng. Let us see what relation subsisted between Roman Pope and Ecumenical Councils in those bright centuries when, as Protestantism in general even now confesses, the Church of Rome professed and taught the pure faith of Christ, and was fitly governed by its own Bishop, with whom all Christendom was bound to agree in faith, and whose teaching all Christendom was under divine obligations of receiving and confessing. Let us examine what the Ecumenical Councils may manifest about the Roman question.

Ecumenical Council! What a tale the words unfold! Greeks, Copts, Nestorians, Jacobites, Eutychians, and Orientals all, and likewise Western Protestant organizations, confess the authority of the Ecumenical Councils of early ages, and admit that no Ecumenical Council can assemble or exist except upon the call and under the presidency of the Bishop of Rome. Ecumenical Council! The expression means Council of the whole world. How significant to a candid-minded thinking believer in Christianity.

XXIII.

A. D. 381, St. Damasus was Bishop of Rome. By order of the Pope a General Council met at Constantinople to take information concerning the Macedonian
heresy. It had been ordered by the Pope that all proceedings should be "sent up" to Rome for final examination and action. A. D. 383, the Pope assembled a
council at Rome where the proceedings of the Constan-
tinopolitan Council were confirmed by a decree of Pope
Damasus, and thus, the assembly of Constantinople was
invested with the name and authority of a General
Council, which, otherwise, it could not possess, for, neither the Pope in person nor his legates had presided
there. The whole programme of the meeting of the
Orientals at Constantinople and the subsequent meeting
of the Western prelates at Rome had been ordered and
pre-arranged by authority of the Roman Pontiff.

A. D. 381, the same year in which was held the Second General Council, one Priscillian, a Manichean, came
from Spain to Rome, "on appeal," to seek absolution
from censures inflicted by a council held at Saragossa,
Spain. Priscillian, to support his infamous teachings
with some show or coloring of authority, had composed,
or had caused to be composed, certain writings bearing
the name of some one or other of the Apostles; and,
also, some, under the names of certain of the old Patriarchs. The Priscillianists had a false Gospel of St.
Matthew. They had added to the books of the New
Testament some false "Acts of St. Thomas," "Acts of
St. Andrew," and "Acts of St. John." They had, more-

over, two other most blasphemous books the names of which this writer does not now recall to mind, and he deems it not of importance to drop his pen for the purpose of searching records. There was much disputing about the books, so that the faithful were exposed to danger of being seduced into error. False brethren, with multiplicity of forged and infamous productions, became distressingly bold, and dangerous to the peace of Christian consciences. The time demanded, and circumstances favored, the promulgation of a decree upon the subject from the only authority on earth competent to define the matter and issue the decree. Pope Damasus, Bishop of Rome, by formal decree A. D. 383, defined the "Canon of Holy Scriptures," giving a catalogue, by name and number, of the books of the Old and New Testaments, as the same, from the days of the Apostles, have been, and now are, received and venerated by the Holy Catholic Church. The Papal decree was, at once, accepted, and every where promulgated throughout the whole Christian world. We notice Bishops giving public testimony of their acceptance of that Papal decree. We read of particular councils giving publicity to an exact catalogue of the sacred books, in manner and form as that catalogue had been received from the Church of Rome. We have chronicles of Councils of Africa, Councils of Gaul, Councils of Spain, and Councils of Italy, the most notable of which are those of Carthage, A. D. 397, and of Toledo, A. D. 402. Exuperius, Bishop of Toulouse, and Decentius, Bishop of Gubbio, ask and receive from Rome the defined catalogue; and the great St. Augustine, Bishop of Hippo Regius, A. D. 400, in his work "On Christian Doctrine," gives an accurate copy of our defined canon. Why all this commotion, so simultaneous, and so general? It was the old story of going up "to see Peter" about an important question of faith—the old story of Peter rising up and defining, and the multitude, afterward, holding their peace. It was according to the Apostolic plan as when, after the decision, St. James rose up and addressed his own flock saying: "Men, brethren, hear me. Peter has spoken and we are the witnesses." *Acts* xv.

All honor and veneration to the glorious old Pope, St. Damasus, thirty-seventh Bishop of Rome, who gave to Christendom, A. D. 383, that infallible decree which defined and fixed forever the "Canon of Holy Scriptures." Every Protestant who reads the "New Testament" and venerates the contents of that sacred compilation, impliedly makes open confession that the Bishop of Rome, fourteen hundred and eighty-eight years ago, was most certainly gifted from Jesus Christ with "Personal Infallibility." The words of Protestantism may pretend to assert otherwise—but facts not words determine our judgment in the premises. Dear "Average," is it not as likely now, A. D. 1871, as it was A. D. 383, that the Pope is "a true and certain witness" of the revelation of Jesus Christ! Answer that question satisfactorily to your own common sense—if you can!

Gentle reader, if you will pardon the writer's seeming prolixity, he will make you familiar with some further details concerning this interesting and very important historical topic. The decree about the "Canon of Scriptures." is sometimes attributed to Pope St. Gelasius, A. D. 494, and sometimes to Pope St. Hormisdas, A. D. 518. English histories and books of controversy—English lecturers and some pulpit speakers, treating the subject matter now under consideration, "go back and stop short" at a particular Council of Carthage, A. D. 397, which council only received recognized and promulgated the decree of the Holy Roman Church, without which authority its own declarations have no weight of absolute and binding certainty.

Pope St. Gelasius, A. D. 494, *did* promulgate a decree, and, with some reference to matters of posterior date, the words of the decree of Gelasius accord with those used by St. Damasus. It is a usual thing to meet with Papal decrees which are more extended re-affirmations of more ancient decrees. The decree of St. Gelasius was one of that kind. Pope St. Hormisdas, A. D. 518, again re-issued the decree with further additions called for by the mooted questions of his own days. The reason why the decree of St. Gelasius acquired the reputation of being the original is easily explained. St. Damasus died A. D. 384; St. Sericius became Pope the same year. From the date of the Supreme Pontificate of St. Sericius we have a continuous series of *official* Papal Acts and Decrees. Official Papal Acts and Decrees of preceding Pontificates did not escape the pillaging destroyers of the early ages. No decrees of St. Damasus, nor of any of his predecessors, are found in the regular series of acts and decrees preserved in the Archives. The decree of St. Gelasius, and that of St. Hormisdas can be found, and, thus, they have come to be looked upon as being the first and the original.

Prove all that! Bless your soul, this "Old Catholic," in these pages, puts forward no statement of any fact which he cannot prove to your heart's content, from "Analytical Treatment of History." If the decree of St. Damasus in council, A. D. 383, be not among the official records in the Archives, for the reason given, that decree *is* extant among ecclesiastical documents. In the manuscripts, it is always found in connection with the "Decree on the Holy Spirit," confirming the proceedings of the Second General Council. All critics without exception are agreed as to the Council at Rome, A. D. 383, wherein the Pope confirmed the decrees of Constantinople. The decree of Pope Damasus is in the collection of manuscripts of that learned and accurate old Abbot, Dionysius the Little, who flourished at Rome about A. D. 500. It is in the collection of Cresconius, A. D. 670. It is in the manuscript collection at St. Mark's, Venice, a manuscript of the eighth century. It is in a manuscript which is possessed by the Cathedral Chapter of Venice, Italy. Moreover, a most ancient manuscript copy of the veritable decree of Pope Damasus, promulgated at the Roman Council, A. D. 383, exists in a manuscript collection in the Library of the Vatican. If the reader shall ever have a desire to bring point blank proof to bear upon the question: "When and by whom was the 'Canon of Holy Scriptures' authoritatively defined and promulgated?"--it may be well to possess the information that the Vatican collection of manuscripts is numbered 5,845. In the manuscripts, after the decree on the Holy Spirit confirming the proceedings of the Second General Council, there follows, immediately, another decree under the following heading: " *We must now treat of the Divine Scriptures ; of that which the Universal Church receives, and of what it ought to avoid.*" Then follows *a decree* in three parts, the first part of which is a " *Catalogue of the books which the Holy Catholic and Roman Church receives and honors.*"

☞ Thus, dear reader, analysis of history demonstrates Holy Damasus, Bishop of Rome, as early as A. D. 383, against Priscillian and other blasphemous corrupters of God's written revelation, defining—infallibly making known to the world—an explicit list of Sacred Books !

XXIV.

A. D. 431, St. Celestine was Bishop of Rome. Nestorius, Archbishop of Constantinople, broached a new heresy, or, rather renewed an old heresy under a new form, concerning the Divine Incarnation. As the rule had been from the days of the earliest disciples, the errors were denounced to the Bishop of Rome. The Pope assembled the Bishops of the West, A. D. 430, and after mature deliberation in their presence, the Pope defined the true Faith and drew up a doctrinal letter on that point of Faith which had been denied. By order of Celestine a General Council met at Ephesus, A. D. 431, *not to discuss*, but *to receive* the Faith, and *to execute the decree* sent to them by the Bishop of Rome. St. Cyril, Patriarch of Alexandria, one of the greatest Prelates of any age, presided at this Third General Council in the name, and by authority of the Pope. St. Celestine dispatched from Rome his legates, bearing with them the doctrinal letter prepared the previous year. That letter was to be presented to St. Cyril and the assembled Bishops, with instructions from the Holy Pontiff of Rome that the cause had been decided, and they were to execute the provisions of the decree, if Nestorius did not retract within the specified time. Here, again, we have the same old practical rule of faith! Peter rose up and spoke, and after Peter had spoken the multitude held their peace. The whole world accepted the teaching of the doctrinal letter of St. Celestine as being a "true and certain" assurance of what really was the revelation of God. The Pope's decree was accepted as Infallible. *Peter had confirmed his brethren!*

14

The words of Pope Celestine to St. Cyril on occasion of this Council are worthy of note: "By authority of the Holy See, and acting in our stead with the power granted to us, you will execute the sentence with exemplary severity." No less noteworthy are the words of the sentence pronounced by the Council: "Nestorius having refused to answer our summons, etc., we have been obliged to enter upon an examination of his impieties. He is convicted on the evidence of his own letters, his writings, and his discourses, etc. Bound by the Holy Canons, and by the letter of our Holy Father Celestine, Bishop of Rome, we are reduced to the necessity of pronouncing this sentence against him, etc. *Bound by the letter of our Holy Father Celestine, Bishop of Rome.*"

The great Bossuet, noticing this sentence of the Third General Council against Nestorius, takes occasion to say that "THE FATHERS RECOGNIZE IN THE POPE'S LETTER THE FORCE OF A JUDICIAL SENTENCE TO WHICH THEY WERE BOUND TO SUBSCRIBE."

Without further comment, and before closing this chapter eighth, we will exhibit another splendid link of our " Golden Chain," the stubborn historical fact of another General Council, only twenty years after this of Ephesus, reiterating the faith of universal christendom about the God-established dogma of Papal Supremacy and Papal Infallibility.

XXV.

FOURTH ECUMENICAL COUNCIL AT CHALCEDON.

A. D. 451, St. Leo the Great was Bishop of Rome and Marcian was Emperor of the East. The Eutychian heresy had disturbed harmony of faith among the Orientals. At the desire of the Pope a Council met at Chalcedon, across the Strait from Constantinople, to restore peace and unity. Through the error of copyists the number of Prelates is variously stated in sundry ancient manuscripts, but the most seemingly correct copies have it that there were six hundred and eighty Bishops in the Assembly. (See Darras' History.) Paschasinus, Bishop of Lillibeum, Lucentius, Bishop of Ascoli, Boniface and Basil, Priests of Rome, presided, by virtue of their office, as Legates of the Bishop of Rome. The first session was held October 8, 451. The Legates opened proceedings by demanding the deposition and exclusion of Dioscorus, Patriarch of Alexandria, because he had had the contumacious audacity to suppress the Pope's letter at a Council held at Ephesus, A. D. 449; and because he had dared to attempt holding a Council without the authority of the Bishop of Rome, "a thing never lawful and never heard of." Dioscorus had presumed to preside in person, as Patriarch of Alexandria, excluding from their official position the Pope's Legates who, as he knew, held in their possession *a doctrinal letter* that condemned the errors to which he was attached. Dioscorus, the first dignitary of the Church next to the Bishop of Rome, was ignored in that great Council of Chalcedon, was deposed, and was forced to retire. The next step in the proceedings was the reading to the Bishops and to the Emperor, *a doctrinal letter* prepared by the Pope, entrusted to the Legates, and addressed to the Bishops and Emperor. The document was a full exposition of Catholic Faith regarding the point which the new heresy attacked. The Council knew its duty— to accept and recognize—not to discuss what the Vicar of Jesus Christ had already defined and decreed.

The unanimous voice of that Grand Council, as a matter of course, accepted the *doctrinal letter* as the dictate of the Holy Ghost, declared it to be the rule of faith throughout the Universal Church, and, with unanimity. of acclamation, the vast assembly cried out aloud : "This is the true Catholic Faith ; Peter hath spoken by Leo." The Fathers present who had assisted at the *Latrocinale* of Ephesus, as it is called in history, and who, under coercion of imperial threats and personal sufferings inflicted by the imperial soldiery, had acquiesced in the doings of the unfortunate Dioscorus, exclaimed aloud that they all had erred, and submissively they declared their repentance and asked pardon.

The great Theodoret, Bishop of Cyrus, a member of the Council, ecclesiastical historian of that age, having heard the reading of *the Pope's doctrinal letter*, rejoiced exceedingly, and thanked God for preserving the Holy Catholic Faith. *Theodoret, Epistle* 121.

Now, this universal acknowledgment of Roman Supremacy and personal Papal Infallibility was exhibited at an historical period when genius would seem to have become an heir-loom to be perpetuated in the bosom of the Holy Catholic Church---and was exhibited by a galaxy of numerous great lights which gave a peculiar splendor to the General Councils assembled during this period, A. D. 325---451.

All this looks something like universally recognized Roman Supremacy and Papal Infallibility, long before the *frigid decrees after A. D.* 1100, about which Martin Luther, not *ignorantly*, but *mendaciously* used to blaspheme.

POPE HORMISDAS AND THE ORIENTALS.

A. D. 518, St. Hormisdas was Bishop of Rome, and Justin I, was Emperor of the East. The Western Roman Empire had been annihilated. The Eastern Empire represented in itself greatness of political power, brilliancy of learning, and splendor of wealth. Mohammed was not yet born. The *temporal* predominance of Rome and of the Pope may be understood from facts narrated by historians of the period, (*Procopius*, b. iii; and others,) that, not long after the date above mentioned, Rome was reduced to a solitude, burnt, and buried in its own ruins. Totila, King of the Goths, carried away with him ALL the inhabitants. For forty days the sun and moon looked down upon the ruins of the city of Augustus, and could discover *not one human creature* in the vicinity. Daniel ii was verified. The stone cut without hands from the mountain had struck the statue upon the feet and had broken it to pieces --preparatory to itself becoming a great mountain to fill the whole earth. Rome used to have four hundred and ten splendid pagan temples, A. D. 410. Alaric plundered the city for three days and then burnt it. Genseric plundered again for fourteen days and then burnt what was remaining. August 23, 476, Odoacer placed upon his own head the crown of Italy, and the Roman Empire of old ceased to exist. Morsels of the Roman territory were parcelled out to a set of barbarians, as each relished the best. So things were until 549, when Totila fulfilled the prophecies as to Pagan Rome. These things are mentioned to show that, in those days, the Bishops of Rome must have dictated the true faith to the powerful Emperors of the East, and to the Bishops and faithful of the world, by an authority far different than could be acquired by prestige of geographical locality or temporal power.

There had been schisms and troubles among the Orientals. Justin and the Prelates of his Dominions wished to secure harmony, and to have security of true faith by returning to communion with the Bishop of Rome. Without an open profession of true orthodox faith none could be in communion with the Pope. From the ruins in Italy a formula of faith emanated to the Orientals. Twenty-five hundred Bishops and other dignitaries of the East, Spiritual Lords Emperor and Temporal Lords, made a public profession of faith, and asked to be received again into the One fold. Of course not all, but only a minority, perhaps a small one at that, had actually followed after error. Here is an extract from the profession of faith sent by the proud Orientals to the man sitting among ruins and devastation—the Successor of St. Peter, who, most likely, had no place to lay his poor afflicted head.

" The words of Christ cannot be passed over, 'Thou art Peter.' In the Apostolic See religion has always been preserved without spot. Therefore we receive all the letters of Pope Leo ; we receive all decrees of the Apostolic See which is THE *perfect and true solidity of the Christian religion.*"

At this period of the Church's history there were about two hundred millions of baptized Catholics, about eight hundred Bishops in Africa and the West, and about one thousand Bishops of Sees in the East. In the East and in Africa the territorial extent of many Episcopal Sees was not great.

XXVII.

SIXTH ECUMENICAL COUNCIL.

A. D. 680, St Agatho was Bishop of Rome, and Constantine Pogonatus—the Bearded—was magnificent Emperor of the East. Politically and socially the Empire of the West—was in fragments. Devastating barbarians from Scandinavia had swept away every vestige of the civilization of preceding ages—except the Catholic Church. She, and her Head the Successor of St. Peter, remained to begin again the work of civilizing the barbarian invaders. In the East there had been trouble, as usual. The Monothelite heresy, a side issue from Arianism, Nestorianism, and Eutychianism, dogmatized against the true faith concerning the Incarnate God. By direction of the Bishop of Rome a General Council assembled at Constantinople to consider the affairs of religion. November 7, 680, the first session was held. Theodore and George, Priests of Rome, and John a Deacon, presided over that Great Council of learned and dignified Bishops and other Magnates, by virtue of their office as Legates of Pope Agatho. The Legates arose and opened the proceedings by reading a "Formula of Faith" drawn up by the Pope, entrusted to the Legates, and addressed to the Bishops and Emperor. In that decretal letter the Pope *defined* the true faith. Rome spoke with authority to the assembled powerful and learned Prelates of the magnificent Eastern Empire and to their mighty Emperor. Not for examination, discussion, or approval, was that "Formula of Faith" submitted by the Bishop of Rome to the Sixth General Council, but for recognition and acceptance. The Council knew its duty full well, and acted accordingly.

He was a grand old Pope, that St. Agatho, speaking from amidst devastations and harrassing inroads of barbarians, telling them of the East, where political greatness and wealth and eloquence flourished, that his Apostolic See was acknowledged by the whole Catholic world to be "the mother and mistress of all other Churches, deriving her authority from St. Peter the Prince of the Apostles, to whom Christ committed his whole flock, with a promise that *his* faith should never fail."

Listen to the words of the Holy Father: "This Apostolic See has never deviated from the truth in any way whatsoever. As it received from its Founder in the beginning, the Chief Apostle of Christ, so it remains untainted to the end, according to the promise of our Lord, ' Simon, Simon, behold Satan hath desired to have *you* that he may sift *you* as wheat, but I have prayed for THEE, that THY faith fail not, and THOU being once converted confirm thy brethren.'" St. Luke, xxii, 31:32. The Holy Pope declares to the representatives of the Christian world, in General Council assembled, that to his See, the Church of Rome, "perfidy never has had access." He excuses the Legates whom he sent to Constantinople for their want of eloquence "because the graces of speech cannot be cultivated amidst the incursions of barbarians, whilst with much difficulty they earned their daily subsistence by the labor of their hands." With sublime simplicity St. Agatho adds this meaningful sentence: "But we preserve the Faith which our Fathers have handed down to us."

They were grand and faithful Catholics, the assembled

Bishops in General Council, by acclamation accepting
the doctrinal letter of St. Agatho as "a rule of faith."
With unanimity of voice which resounded all over the
Christian world that Sixth General Council proclaimed:
"This is the Catholic Faith; this is the Faith of our
Fathers; Peter hath spoken by Agatho."

The Council lasted ten months, and held eighteen sessions. There was no thought of deciding upon what
was the true faith of Christ by the principle of a majority vote in those true Christian days of "auld lang
syne." The plan established by Jesus himself was well
known, and rigidly followed.

☞ Dear and candid reader, please ponder the strong
words subscribed to by every member of that Sixth General Council, in reply to the Apostolic Brief of Pope St.
Agatho, and then form for yourself an opinion of the
men who boldly assert that the Greeks never acknowledged the supremacy, by divine right, of the Bishop of
Rome. Here are the words: "Christ, our true God,
hath given us a wise physician, even your Holiness,
honored of God, who firmly repellest the contagious
plague of heresy and impartest the strength of health
to all the members of the Church. To *thee*, therefore,
as the First See of the Universal Church, standing upon
the firm rock, we leave what is to be done, having read
the letter of a true confession sent by your paternal
blessedness, which letter we recognize as divinely written
from the Supreme Head of the Apostles." *Mansi*, xi,
239, 683. No set form of words could more decidedly
express recognition of Roman Supremacy and Papal Infallibility. Reader dear, how thinkest thou?

XXVIII.

EIGHTH GENERAL COUNCIL.

A. D. 869, Adrian II was Bishop of Rome and Basil
the Macedonian was Emperor of Constantinople. By

authority of the Pope a summoned General Council met in the great Church of St. Sophia at Constantinople.

On the fifth day of October, A. D. 869, the first session commenced, and through ten sessions the Fathers cooly and deliberately treated the subject of religion, finishing their debates Feb. 28, A. D. 870. Donatus, Bishop of Ostia, Stephen, Bishop of Nepi, and Marinus, one of the seven deacons of Rome, presided in their official capacity as Legates of Adrian II, Bishop of Rome. St. Ignatius, Patriarch of Constantinople, sat next to the deputies of the three Oriental Patriarchs of Alexandria Antioch and Jerusalem. Here we have Universal Christendom represented in General Council. The Emperor was present as a spectator. It was a solemn occasion. The Legates arose and commenced proceedings. It was agreed that the first thing in order should be the reading of a " Formulary of Faith " which the Legates had brought with them from the Bishop of Rome, the Supeme Head of the Universal Church, who was too far advanced in age, and too feeble to be there present in person. The Formulary of Faith was read, and, by acclamation, universally recognized and accepted. A Council had been held the previous year, A. D. 868, at Rome. The Western Bishops had decreed as follows : " If any one despise the dogmas, commandments, or decrees in respect to Catholic Faith promulgated by the Holy Roman Pontiff who presides, let him be anathema." That decree of the Western Bishops assembled at Rome, A. D. 868, was, the following year, presented to the assembled Orientals. The Eighth General Council recognized, and with all becoming formality accepted, that plain decree above given. All proceedings were approved and confirmed by the Head of the Church, Pope Adrian the Second.

XXIX.

ECUMENICAL COUNCIL AT LYONS.

A. D. 1274, Gregory X was Bishop of Rome. The East had "seceded," A. D. 1053, and now sighed for "reconstruction." By order of Pope Gregory a General Council assembled at Lyons, France. The first session was held May 7, 1274. There were present five hundred Bishops, seventy Abbots, about one thousand other dignitaries, and the ambassadors of the Kings of England, France, Sicily, and the German Princes. The Pope in person presided.

On the sixth of July, during the fourth session, the Greeks approached the city of Lyons with a view of petitioning for a re-union with the Holy Catholic Church. All the Latin Prelates went out to meet the Greeks. The Eastern strangers were conducted in procession by the Latin Prelates and presented to the Holy Father, who, bathed in tears, received the returning schismatics with all that feeling exhibition of soul-moving charity and joy which one might expect from the representative on earth of Jesus Christ. The Greek delegation was composed of thirty-six Archbishops with their respective suffragans. The ambassadors of the Emperor, Michael Paleologus, were, Germanus who had been Patriarch of Constantinople, Theophanes, Archbishop of Nice, and George Acropolita, Chancellor of the Empire. In the name of the Emperor the Chancellor abjured the schism and addressed the Holy Father as " First Supreme Pontiff." The Archbishops and Bishops saluted the Vicar of Jesus Christ, Bishop of Rome, by the title of great and excellent Pontiff of the Apostolic See. The profession of faith which all the Greeks subscribed at Lyons has the following words: "The Holy Roman Church holds supreme and full Primacy and Headship over the whole Catholic Church, which she truly and humbly acknowledges herself to have received from the Lord himself, in the person of blessed Peter, the Prince and Head of the Apostles, whose successor is the Roman Pontiff, with the plenitude of power. And as before all others she is bound to defend the truth, also, if any questions arise concerning the faith, they ought by her judgment to be defined. By mouth and heart we confess that which the sacred and Holy Roman Church truly holds and faithfully teaches and preaches." *Mansi*, xxiv, 71. Roman Supremacy and Papal Infallibility again! And that, too, in words which cannot be mistaken. What a sublime scene did the city of Lyons exhibit on the ninth day of June, A. D. 1274! The Bishop of Rome, in person, presiding over a General Council composed of not less than two thousand ecclesiastical dignitaries from the East and from the West, Greeks and Latins! The eyes of the whole civilized world were fixed upon that assembly. The Eastern Emperor, the Kings of England, France and Sicily, also the Princes of the German Empire, were present by their accredited proxies. Then and there, united Christendom, with not one dissenting voice, made and placed upon record a free and bold recognition---not of a novelty, but of the ancient faith regarding Supremacy and Infallibility of St Peter's successor. Our authorities are no " Isidorian decretals," no *forged* or *frigid* decrees!

All our statements are statements of true historical facts---stubborn facts --attested by documents the authenticity of which no real scholar ever ventured to dispute.

Yea, verily! and there stands the poor man, Herr Von Dœllinger, in the face of the world, with chalk, tape line, and shears, like a tailor, trying to *clip* and *trim* history to make it "a good fit" for his pet costomer, *Cæsarism.*

Kind reader, this writer leaves it to you to decide if there be not, in the professor's attempts, a great waste of time and cloth, and no *fit* after all. The excellent lady correspondent from Rome of the *Freeman's Journal,* in a late letter, suggests to us a striking illustration which we beg to set forth in our own words and style. A zealous Methodist preacher *converted* a ragged Catholic boy by a new jacket and trowsers, and would make a display of the *take.* On the following *Sabbath,* so called, boy stood before preacher, and congregation sat to be edified. The scene opened: PREACHER--"Boy, can you say any prayers?" BOY---"I can sir. Hail Mary, full of grace"--"Hold on there, boy, we want no such popish *innovation* and *novelty* here about your Virgin Mary! Can't you say the *Apostles' Creed,* which all orthordox Protestant Christians are accustomed to repeat, as the first Christians used to do?" "I can sir! I Believe in God the Father Almighty, Creator of heaven and earth; and in Jesus Christ, His only Son, our Lord, who was conceived by the Holy Ghost, born of the Virgin Mary! O, Sir, there she is again! What are you going to do about it now?" Alas, poor Dœllinger! Alas, *thy* "Analytical Treatment of History!"

XXX.

ECUMENICAL COUNCIL AT CONSTANCE.

A. D. 1414, Gregory XII was Bishop of Rome. He was, including St. Peter, in a direct, legitimate, unbroken line, the two hundred and fifth Pope, Vicar on earth of Jesus Christ. At this period the minds of many seem to have been wonderfully bewildered about the claims to the Papacy of certain personages who are sometimes designated as doubtful Popes, as if Jesus Christ ever did, or, according to his divine promises, ever could permit His Holy Church to be given over to the guidance of a *doubtful* Head. It falls not within the scope of this treatise to discuss the situation of ecclesiastical affairs as then existing. Our only purpose is to show that the evidences of Roman Supremacy or Papal Infallibility never, from the day of Christ's Ascension, suffered historical eclipse.

An assembly of Christendom met at Constance, A. D. 1414, to take into consideration the case of pretenders to the Papacy, but the question of Supremacy or Infallibility of the Successor of St. Peter was neither discussed nor mooted. "PAPA ELECTUS NON POTEST LIGARI;" "*A Pope once elected is subject to no action of a Council,*" was the universal exclamation of all Christendom—excepting a few of the "Old Sorbonne," who would have affairs of the Universal Church regulated in subserviency to the human interests of French and English national policy. An insignificant faction headed by the learned and famous John Gerson, Chancellor of the Paris University, under the ostensible pretence of meeting the peculiar exigencies of the times, *invented* and used to talk about a pet theory, about which no Christian save John and his few companions had ever dreamed. The faction would weaken the authority of the Holy See by introducing and agitating the question *whether the Pope is superior to a General Council, or a General Council to the Pope.* The very statement of the question presents an inadmissible hypothesis. To discuss the question on an acceptable ground it would be necessary to find a General Council acting without the Pope, or a Pope standing apart from a General Council. But the *two* ideas are *contradictory*. No Council, it is admitted on all hands, can be Ecumenical without the Pope. No argument can, therefore, be formed on the hostile attitude of the two powers when, by the very fact of their separation, one (the Council) must cease to exist. See our numbered propositions set forth in this pamphlet, pp. 14, 15 and 19, 20; and ponder well *proposition* 3, p. 14, the assumed illustrative case of "the Pope, the fifty, and the five hundred." See also M. De Maistre *On the Pope*, and Darras, vol. i, c. 7.

There was a vast assemblage of ecclesiastical and temporal magnates at Constance, A. D. 1418, and truth of history demonstrates that the novelty and pet theory of Gerson and his petty handful of French courtiers received, outside of their own little French tent, a very contemptuous reception. Gregory XII, on the 4th of July, 1415, to facilitate and hasten a return of harmony and peace, resigned the Papal office, of which he was the rightful incumbent as no one denies, and on the eleventh day of November, 1417, Martin V was elected Bishop of Rome, Supreme Pontiff, Pope, which termination of preceding schismatical troubles gave universal joy to Christendom. AFTER THAT ELECTION the Council of Constance, presided over by the Pope in person, was an ECUMENICAL COUNCIL--not sooner. The acts of the last four sessions—together with such acts of preceding sessions as the Pope saw fit to confirm—are the only Pope-approved authoritative binding proceedings of the celebrated Ecumenical Council called the Council of Constance. It is a matter of very little importance what the little coterie of French, collectively or individually, thought or said about their pet scheme, but it is a matter of very great importance what an Ecumenical Coun-

cil did decree and promulgate. Behold a fact! It is
Conciliar evidence of the most decided kind. In the last
session of the Council, the Poles, because the Pope would
not condemn a certain book, appealed to a future General Council. Martin V, in a public consistory, on the
10th day of March, 1418, condemned all such appeals.
The confirmed decree of that great Council of Constance
runs in these words:

"It is lawful to no one to appeal from the Supreme
Judge, namely, the Apostolic See, or the Roman Pontiff,
the Vicar, on earth, of Jesus Christ, or TO REVERSE HIS
JUDGMENTS IN CAUSES OF FAITH, which, as *causæ majores*,
are to be referred to him and the Apostolic See."

If that decree be not strong and manifest Conciliar
recognition of Roman Supremacy and Papal Infallibility,
we are at a loss to understand the requisites of plainly
worded evidence. How ridiculous it is for opponents
of Catholicity and maligners of Papacy to exhibit themselves as murderers of historical truth----putting forth as
"enactments of the General Council of Constance" certain unsupported assertions which true history notes as
only stage "*asides*" of interested French actors.

All scholars of note admit John Gerson's vast profundity of learning, and his distinguished intellectual
ability to analyze history. The above cited condemnation of an "appeal from Pope to Council" was not pleasing to a man who had invented a contrary pet theory.
John wrote against the condemnation, and, in order to
make his case---to find if possible some semblance of
ancient authority in favor of his hobby--all the literary
monuments of Christian antiquity were subjected to a
most rigid investigation. In the domain of literature
John Gerson, in comparison with Luther, Dœllinger,

and Cincinnati pulpit infidels, must be regarded as a Drummond light compared with so many "tallow dips." But John's search was in vain. John himself tells his experience, and one can perceive the chagrin of a disappointed man by his fling of the disrespectful word "pedant" at the whole brilliant array of Saints and Doctors of the preceding fourteen centuries. Hear John's evidence, given after the Council of Constance:—"If I am not mistaken, before the celebration of the Holy Council of Constance, this tradition—that decisions of a Pope cannot be appealed—had so possessed the minds of pedants rather than lettered men, that any one who should have dogmatically taught the opposite would have been noted and condemned for heretical pravity." *Gerson's works, tome* 1, p. 303, ed. Antwerp, 1706. The remarkably learned divine, Theophilus Raynaud, whose works were published in twenty tomes, Cracow, 1669, gives a faithful portraiture of the situation as existing prior to the Constancian Council: "It is in vain now to bring up a lot of theologians, since *all* may be adduced who lived before the Council of Constance. This truth of the indefectibility of the Roman Pontiff and Roman See *was never called in question.* All who went before invariably taught that the definitions of the Pontiff without a General Council made matter of faith—that every judgment of faith belonged authoritatively to the Holy See." For more abundant testimonies with plain references to original authorities, book and page, one may consult some admirable papers from the pen of the amiable and deeply read Archbishop Manning of Westminster, published in the January 1870 numbers of the *New York Freeman's Journal.*

Our space and scope forbid further quotations or comments, other than inviting attention to three or four his-

torical facts which are worthy of a serious pondering.
1. The much talked-about Council of Constance, as evi-
denced by the above *unanimous decree*, recognized and confessed Roman Supremacy and Papal ,Infallibility, with
equally emphatic distinctness as did any individual,' or
Council, of the preceding fourteen hundred years. 2. Before the time of this Council, there never was in Christendom,. from any source .deserving of even a passing
notice, denial of, or protest against, the said Papal prerogatives. Evidence of such denial or protest has never
been produced, and never can be produced. 3. The pet
theory of a few French courtiers had precious little influence upon the Christian public mind, as may be dis-
cerned from proceedings of another Ecumenical Council,
held at Florence a few years afterward, whilst numbers
of the men of Constance were yet living. 4. As the
whole Catholic world now smiles with pity at the silly
twaddle of so-called "Ministers of the Gospel," and at
ignorant pen-droppings of "editors" and "own specials,"
about Dœllinger and his "new departure," so in those
days of the Council of Constance, and afterward, the
whole Catholic world, including even the great majority
of Doctors in France, including all, in fact, except the
few interested *inventors*,---Doctors not only in theology
but also in law---following the truth which had founda-
tions impossible to be destroyed, "*laughed at the opinion
of the " Old Sorbonne.*"

Peter de Marca, Archbishop of Paris, A. D. 1661, is
responsible for the substance of the above declaration
about the "French Doctors," and for the ipsissima italic
words with which the paragraph concludes. *Zaccaria*,
diss. 5, c. 2., edit. Rom., 1843. Down to the time of
Peter de Marca,. "Catholic Theology" influenced *France*.
Not yet had that "Oldest Daughter of the Catholic

Church " felt the damning effects of that " Royal Theology " which prepared the way for the fiendish horrors of 1792 and 1871. The well known Catholic faith of France, before Louis XIV tried to make himself "The Church," in like manner as he declared of himself, "I am the State," "L'ETAT C'EST MOI," may be understood from this little fact of history, to-wit: " The leading Jansenists held a meeting in the FAUBOURG ST. JACQUES on the publication of the Bull of Innocent X. The renowned Pascal suggested that he had HEARD that the Pope is not infallible. The leader of the Jansenist leaders, Arnauld, immediately answered that if they should pursue THAT line of defence, "*they would give good reason to their opponents to treat them as heretics.*" *Bouix, de Papa*, p. 503. Papal Infallibility a novelty! No indeed, dear reader, not even in France! How can the Catholic world help smiling with pity at the gullibility which so readily takes upon trust " ministerial " and " editorial " salary-drawing fiction. Truthful history " about Pope and popery," from anti-Catholic pulpit or press, would'nt pay! No, indeed!

XXXI.

ECUMENICAL COUNCIL AT FLORENCE.

A. D. 1437 Eugenius IV was Bishop of Rome. The human causes which produced and reproduced "secession " of the perfidious Greeks from Catholic Unity are not difficult of comprehension. We have neither space nor time nor wish to enter upon an explanation. After the re-union of A. D. 1274, we find them again, in a body, Prelates Emperor and Magnates, A. D. 1439, "going to confession " to the Pope, declaring sincere sorrow for their crime, promising permanent fidelity for the future, and asking pardon, absolution, and re-admission into communion with the Supreme Head of the One Fold of Jesus Christ. John Paleologus IV, Emperor of Constantinople, the venerable Joseph, Patriarch of Constantinople, Archbishops, Bishops, and Grandees, addressed themselves to Pope Eugenius, with proposals for a return of the Greeks to the Catholic Church. Arrangements progressed satisfactorily, and, with becoming submissiveness, they came "to See Peter."

The time is July 6, 1439. The place is Florence, Italy. Friendly reader, let us enter the magnificent Cathedral. A General Council has been sitting for more than eighteen months. It is now holding its tenth session, the last session at Florence. The Pope himself presides. Latins and Greeks, with approval of the Pope, have agreed to the re-union. A decree has been formed. The renowned Cardinal Julian reads the "decree of union" in Latin, and the celebrated Bessarion reads the same in Greek. The Churches of Rome and Constantinople, the whole East and the whole West, are united in profession of the same One Faith, under One Visible Supreme Head of Christ's Church,---"the Bishop of Rome, commonly called the Pope," as our little Catechism expresses the title.

The Pope, first, and all the Latin Fathers, the Emperor, next, and all the Greeks, except alone Mark of Ephesus, sign the "decree of union." The profession of faith required of the Greeks is the very same as that professed by their venerated predecessors in the earliest Christian ages--the very same as that professed at Nice, Sardica, Chalcedon, Ephesus---the very same as that which Polycarp, Irenæus, John Chrysostom, and the Popes St. Leo, St. Hormisdas, St. Agatho, and Adrian, used to teach earlier Greeks of purest orthodox times.

The decree of union, unanimously agreed to and signed by Greeks and Latins, confirmed and announced by the Pope, had these words: "In the name of the Holy Trinity, Father, Son, and Holy Ghost, by the approbation of this Sacred and Ecumenical Council, assembled at Florence, we define:--That in the Apostolic See and Roman Pontiff resides the Primacy over the whole earth, that the Roman Pontiff is the successor of St. Peter, Chief of the Apostles, and the true Vicar of Christ, the Head of the Church, the Father and TEACHER of all Christians, and ·that to him, in the person of St. Peter, was given by Jesus Christ PLENITUDE OF POWER to feed, to direct, and to govern the Universal Church, as is contained in the acts of the Ecumenical Councils and in the Sacred Canons."

The same year, A. D. 1439, on the twenty-second day of November, the same Pope, Eugenius IV, received to Catholic Union the repentant Armenians, whose Bishops and Magnates, in like manner as the Greeks, had journeyed from the distant Orient " to see Peter." The profession of faith to which the Armenian Orientals subscribed adhesion was in perfect accord with that signed by the Greeks.

An estimable recent convert to Catholicity, James Kent Stone, S. T. D., late President of Kenyon College, Gambier, Ohio, and of Hobart College, Geneva, New York, in his learned work, *The Invitation Heeded*, p. 331, has these excellent remarks : " It is an interesting fact, and may yet prove, in the good Providence of God, a most blessed fact, that the grandest testimonies to the Infallibility of the Holy See, have been given by Councils in which the Greeks have borne a conspicuous part. It seems as though they were brought to Lyons and to Florence with a divine purpose, that they might join in re-affirming the ancient truth which their forefathers confessed at Ephesus, at Chalcedon, and at Constantinople. And when they return at last to the fold from which they have so often strayed, they will have no new faith to learn, but only the old faith to repeat."

XXXI.

ECUMENICAL COUNCILS OF LATERAN AND TRENT.

A. D. 1512, a Council was summoned by Pope Julius II. It assembled April 19, 1512. Julius died before the termination of business. Leo X continued the sessions and presided in person. Session eleventh was held December 19, 1516. The fourth item of interest in the record of that session is a plainly worded recognition of "plenitude of power in the Roman Pontiff over all Councils ; a right which is according to ancient custom, and acknowledged by preceding Councils." This Council terminated with its twelfth session, March 16, 1517. Pope Leo X solemnly confirmed all its decrees.

A. D. 1545, the great Council of Trent commenced its sessions, December 13, and closed them at the end of the year 1563. January, 1564, Pope Pius IV confirmed the decrees of this Council, which had continued its sessions, with interruptions, during eighteen years, and under five successive Popes. The doctrinal decisions of this Ecumenical Council differ, in absolutely nothing, from the invariable teachings of the Catholic Church since the days of the Council of Jerusalem, A. D. 49, or 51. That Council, too, in no less than four places, intimates Roman Supremacy and Infallibility, though no decree was made, because the question was not introduced for treatment in any formal manner.

Sessions VII, XIV, XXII, XXV, describe the Roman

Church as "Ecclesiarum omnium Mater et Magistra." The word "Magistra" signifies the authority to
teach and guide. The reader will please understand
that our English expressions do not adequately convey
to one's mind that full force of meaning which the original Latin terms imply. A classical scholar can appreciate the inadequacy of our weak mode of rendering the
"Summum Magisterium" of the Council of Florence,
and the "Magistra" of the Council of Trent. We
may illustrate by reference to the *original* words of the
commission which Jesus addressed to Peter; "feed my
lambs," "feed my sheep," *St. John*, xxi.. As written by
the Evangelist, the word which we translate *feed* has a
much wider signification than the poverty of our language can express in any corresponding one word.
Poimaine ta Probata Mou is the sentence as it came
from the Apostolic pen. In Homeric language, Poimaine is applicable to the highest prerogative of royalty
--feed, govern, teach, protect, etc. Homer's Poimen
Laon is a kingly appellation. This writer would suggest *supreme care-taker* as something as near to the true
translation as our language will allow. It is worthy of
remark that Jesus Christ, *St. John*, x, calls Himself
Poimen of the sheep of His own fold, and when He
was about to leave the earth He constituted Peter His
Vicar,---the words of the commission expressing that Peter was to be regarded as Supreme *care-taker* of Christ's
lambs and sheep. The Evangelist uses the same kingly
manner of speech, with regard to Christ and to Peter!
Boskein is the Greek original for which our word *feed*
is an equivalent. Kenrick's *Primacy*, and James Kent
Stone's *Invitation Heeded*, give lengthy notes on the remarkable significance of the kingly term which Christ
used of Himself, and addressed to Peter. Our apprecia-

tion of Scripture expressions must be based, not upon what translated words in modern languages may *seem* to mean, but upon what the actual words that were used and written were intended to mean, and *did* mean.

XXXII.

ECUMENICAL COUNCIL OF THE VATICAN.

A. D. 1869, Pius IX, Bishop of Rome, our present Sovereign Pontiff, on the twenty-ninth day of June, issued an Apostolic Brief summoning an Ecumenical Council to convene at the Vatican on the festival of the IMMACULATE CONCEPTION, December 8, 1869. At the solemn opening of the Council the Pope was saluted by EIGHT HUNDRED AND TWENTY-SEVEN Patriarchs, Metropolitans, and Bishops, from all parts of the world, to say nothing of the great number of Cardinals, heads of Religious Orders, Eminent Consultive Theologians, and conciliar officials of various titles. During the early days of the great Vatican Council, about SIX HUNDRED BISHOPS presented for consideration and action a subscribed *Postulatum*, or what an American would call a Petition. The document of the Six Hundred Bishops is a very plain and full statement of the question of "Papal Infallibility," as proposed for definition to the assembled Fathers of the First Vatican Ecumenical Council. Our generous readers, doubtless, will be pleased to peruse and ponder the document itself. Here is a faithful English translation:—

POSTULATUM OF THE BISHOPS.

"The Fathers humbly and earnestly beg of the Sacred Ecumenical Vatican Synod, that it will be pleased to decree, in clear words, and to the exclusion of every room for doubt, that the authority of the Roman Pontiff, IN MATTERS OF FAITH AND MORALS, when he ordains and prescribes those things which are to be believed, or those which are to be rejected and condemned by all the faithful Christians, is Supreme, and therefore exempt from error."

REASONS IN SUPPORT OF THE OPPORTUNENESS AND NECESSITY OF THE DECREE.

" The Holy Scriptures plainly teach that the Roman Pontiff, the successor of St. Peter, has the primacy of jurisdiction, and also of SUPREME MAGISTERIUM, over the whole Church of Christ.

" The universal and constant teaching of the Church, set forth by the Fathers, and by Councils of all kinds, proclaims, as well in acts as in language, that the judgments of the Roman Pontiff on doctrines of faith and morals are irreformable.

" The profession of faith adopted with the consent of Greeks and Latins, in the Second General Council of Lyons, A. D. 1274, declared that all controversies on matters of faith must be decided by the judgment of the Roman Pontiff.

" The Ecumenical Synod of Florence DEFINED that the Roman Pontiff is the Vicar of Christ, the Head of the whole Church ; the Father and Teacher of all Christians ; that to him in the person of St. Peter PLENITUDE OF POWER was given by our Lord Jesus Christ, to feed, to rule, to govern the Universal Church. Sound reason shows that no one can be in a position of communion with the Church without agreeing with her head, since the Church cannot lawfully be separated, even in thought, from the head.

" There have been, and there are still some who call themselves Catholics, and who turn their use of that name into the destruction of weaker brethren, by presuming to teach that THE DECISIONS OF THE POPE NEED ONLY BE RECEIVED WITH A RESPECTFUL SILENCE, without any interior assent—and subject to the ulterior assent of the Church. Every one sees that this perverse doctrine tends to overthrow the authority of the Pope, to scatter the unity of the faith, to open the doors to errors, and to give them time to spread.

" Moved by these considerations, many Bishops have of late exerted themselves to cause the true doctrine to be proclaimed by synodal decrees, and by general testimony, but the more zealously the truth has. been set forth, the more vehement has become the clamor, directed to excite the people against sound doctrine, and even to deter the Council of the Vatican from defining the same. Men who call themselves Catholics have published attacks against the Holy See, and have dared to affirm that the Council of Florence, which so plainly set forth the supreme authority of the Roman Pontiff, was not an Ecumenical Council.

"Therefore, if the OPPORTUNESS of the definition of the true doctrine by the Council of the Vatican was ever doubtful, it is now quite clear that hesitation is no longer possible. If, this Council were to be silent on the subject, and to neglect to bear testimony of the truth after such provocation, that truth would really begin to be doubted by true Catholics; and the adversaries would boastingly assert that they had by their arguments silenced the Council. Such silence would be abused by the disobedient, as an excuse for open resistence to the judgments and decrees of the Holy See. On these grounds the Fathers urge the Council to make the decree set forth in the petition.

"The Fathers respectfully refer to the idea entertained by a few of their venerable fellow conciliars—that the definition ought to be indefinitely postponed, 'not because the doctrine is not and has not always been true and recognized by the Universal Church, but lest schismatics and heretics should, by a plain outspoken definition of the truth, be driven farther from the Church. Not being prepared in mind to understand the precise purport, nature, and extent of the doctrine, certainly true in itself, there will be difficulty in maintaining the dogma by proofs to their satisfaction. Deep seated prejudice and bigotry will be aroused afresh—and there will be ' an end to conversions from among intelligent Protestants.'

"To the INOPPORTUNISTS it is replied, in the first place, that the faithful have a right to claim the teaching of the Ecumenical Council, on so grave a doctrine, after the doctrine has been so industriously attacked, lest, hereafter, the minds of many should be corrupted by pernicious error. It is also further replied that the Council of Lyons, and other Councils, were not deterred by any such considerations or apprehensions, from declaring and establishing right doctrine. It is further replied that sincere searchers for truth will not be driven away, but rather will be attracted by the plain precise definition of the chief foundation upon which the unity and solidity of the Catholic Church repose. It is yet again replied that intelligent Protestants, the more intelligent they are, the more they will cast aside prejudices of education, and rise superior to the littleness of bigotry; the more intelligent they are, the more they will bring the native force and power of unclouded reason to investigate and learn if these things be so—if the doctrine proclaimed so plainly, and so openly, be really and truly a fact, and thus there will NOT be 'an end to conversions from among intelligent Protestants.'

" It is respectfully set forth, that if any persons be really driven from the Church by the definition, those alone will come to this end who are already opposed to the Church in their interior minds, and are only waiting for a pretext to separate themselves from her by exterior action. These are the very men against whom the duty of the Vatican Council compels it to guard the faithful children of the Catholic Church.

" The faithful children of the Catholic Church, with joyful acclamation, will receive a reiterated plain authoritative declaration, that in teaching *ex cathedra*—officially—matters of faith and morals to the Universal Church—the Roman Pontiff is, by divine influence, not capable of erring—IS INFALLIBLE."

The above *Postulatum* to the Sacred Ecumenical Council of the Vatican, subscribed and presented by about three fourths of the Bishops there assembled, displays an unmistakable historical fact with regard to the whole subject matter of Papal Infallibility, as the same was considered and acted upon by the said Council. The designed purpose, most happily accomplished, was to dispel most thoroughly, and forever, the hazy mists of seeming obscurity which interested worldlings, sycophants of Cæsarism more particularly, pretended to discover, and fain would take advantage of, in certain verbal expressions sometimes used in preceding times. It has been only in our own days that the dogma of Papal Infallibility has been systematically assailed; it is, therefore, very becoming that, in our days, that dogma should be specifically *defined*. A decree was formed July 18, 1870, and was duly promulgated by the Holy Father Pope Pius IX. The heading of that decree is a plain indication of the fullest meaning of " Papal Infallibility as defined by the Vatican Council" about which Dr. Dœllinger and a few others would cause dissension among Catholics—if they could. This is the heading :—
OF THE OFFICE OF THE POPE AS INFALLIBLE TEACHER.

The Ecumenical Council defined *anew* the dogma of Papal Infallibility, but the Council did not,---could not -- define a *new* dogma. The Vatican Council defined *anew* the ancient dogma, that is, explained the dogma with precision, and exhibited its meaning clearly and with exactness, as the great " Unabridged " defines to us the word "define." Some Zealous, learned, and holy Prelates, before the definition, entertained and expressed, as they had a right to do, peculiar views about the " opportuneness" of agitating the point of personal Papal Infallibility at this time, but the question of the truth of the dogma itself was not thought of as a matter of discussion. How could it? Does not our *Catena Aurea* demonstrate from " Analytical Treatment of History," that a denial of Papal Infallibility logically involves a denial of the Divinity of Jesus Christ? It consequently involves a denial of the truth of Christianity, and; in fact, a denial of all divine revelation from God to man. Does not *Catena Aurea* exhibit the Holy Catholic Christian Church, from the day of Christ's Ascension even until the Vatican definition, recognizing 'and proclaiming the dogma in terms most emphatic? There has been no tremor in her voice; through the long centuries it has sounded like a ceaseless thunder !"

No, indeed! friendly reader, there was no shadow of doubt in the mind of any one Bishop of the Catholic Church, in the year of our Lord 1870, about the absolute truth of the dogma of Papal Infallilbility as defined and held in preceding ages!---and, since it hath seemed good to the Holy Ghost and to the Sacred Ecumenical Council of the Vatican to pronounce upon the question of " opportuneness," the opinion called " inopportuneness " is never heard from lips of faithful Catholics. In this wide wide world there is not existing one Bishop of the Holy Catholic Church who is not in perfect accord with every other Bishop, and ALL in most perfect accord with the Supreme Pontiff, Bishop of Rome, with regard to all doctrines of divine faith, and particularly with regard to the doctrine of personal Papal Infallibility.

In the Council of the Vatican we discover the identical mode of proceeding which we find recorded of the Council of Jerusalem, *Acts* xv. There was much disputing about "opportuneness," and then Peter stood up and defined. And when Peter had spoken all the multitude held their peace. The Bishops, immediately afterterward, each in his own See, rose up and addressed his own respective flock, saying, after the manner of James at Jerusalem: Men, brethren, Peter hath spoken by Pius, and we were there as witnesses! The Catholic Church, judging and decreeing about points of divine faith, has never deviated from the plan which was instituted by Jesus Christ, and which was taught and acted upon by the Apostles themselves.

The author, purposely, has refrained from adding to his "Golden Chain of Evidences," the testimonies of individual Fathers, Doctors, or other writers, since the days when the Church began to speak forth in Ecumenical Council. Declaration of particular councils are not noticed. The "chain" might be made longer, but could gain nothing in strength. Every one understands that, in the successive centuries, a WHOLE body deposing unanimously, and with authority, is more demonstrative of a FACT than is, or can be, the opinion of this or that individual part of the body. We can and shall, however, in a nutshell as it were, demonstrate the individual testimonies of all noteworthy Fathers, Doctors, Theologians and orthodox ecclesiastical writers. On our next page ONE shall speak for ALL.

St. Thomas, of Aquin, of the Order of St. Dominic, died March 7, A. D. 1274, and was solemnly canonized A. D. 1323. The Catholic Church has always recognized St. Thomas as a faithful interpreter of St. Augustine, St. Gregory the Great, in fine, as being a condensing ORACLE of the teachings of all the Fathers, Doctors, and ecclesiastical writers who preceded him. Since his day, he has been universally regarded as an authoritative STANDARD of reference regarding all points of Catholic Faith. When the Holy Council of Trent assembled, there was placed in the centre of the assembly a table upon which stood a splendid representation of Jesus Christ crucified. On the same table, on one side of the crucifix, the Fathers caused to be placed a copy of the Holy Bible, and on the other side a copy of the *Summa* of St. Thomas, of Aquin, for convenience of reference during the discussions. That historical fact is a sufficient demonstracion of the importance and weight which Christendom has always given to the evidence of St. Thomas, of Aquin, on points of Catholic faith.

The *Summa* of St. Thomas, 2, 2, q. 1, a. 1, and his *Opuscul.* vi., De Symb. Apost., declare as follows : "Therefore the Lord said to Peter, whom he made Supreme Pontiff, I have prayed for THEE, that THY faith fail not, and THOU, when thou art converted, confirm thy brethren. And of this, the reason is, that the faith of the whole Church must be ONE, which cannot be so kept unless questions of faith be determined by him who presides over the whole Church, so that his judgment and sentence be held by the whole Church"---" while in other parts there is either no faith, or it is mingled with many errors, the Church of Peter is fresh in faith, and pure from error, and no wonder, because the Lord said, I have prayed for THEE that THY faith fail not."

CHAPTER ELEVENTH.

XXXIII.

PROTESTANTISM COMBINED, A. D. 1530, RECOGNIZED PAPAL INFALLIBILITY.

Protestantism was born into this world seven months and a half after the close of the last General Council of Lateran. At the time of its birth there was not in all Christendom a dissenting voice against recognition of "plenitude of power in the Roman Pontiff over all Councils." It must not be forgotten that, to this day, the schismatic Greeks and other Eastern separatists confess their inability to hold a General Council, because such a Council must be called and presided over by the Patriarch of Rome, according to the ancient canons which they revere. What was the faith of new born Protestantism about the tenet of Papal Infallibility? Why, bless you, Protestantism was not established for the purpose of having faith about anything! It was instituted, solely, to *protest* against faith. The essence of Protestantism is to *protest* against faith, not to *have* it. If we now find it loudly protesting against Papal Infallibility, there can be no better proof in the world that " Papal Infallibility is no novelty."

Martin Luther, D. D., of Wittemberg, Germany, was "*inspired*" at midnight, October 31, 1517, to affix to the outer pillars of *All Saints Church*, the famous "ninety-five propositions."

The tares were sown in befitting soil; the sprouts came up and began to shoot forth in the eden of the Church, baneful weeds of every noxious description. The *alleged* first cause of Luther's new departure from the Church of Christ was the *teachings of the Church regarding the doctrine of indulgences.*

The "young idea," afterward called Protestantism, was the pet offspring and pupil of *inspired* (?) Luther. Here is the first lesson which the *inspired* parent and heavenly minded master developed into the tender, enquiring, craving mind of "young idea:" "Upon my salvation, at the time I put up those propositions, I knew no more what an indulgence was, than did those who came to enquire of me." *Luther's Works*, tome vii, page 462, Altenberg edition. Pretty candid acknowledgment that! coming as it did from an *inspired* man. He would introduce a new theory regarding a point of ancient doctrine, knowing no more about that point of doctrine, than did his most ignorant hearers. It was not thus that God sent Moses, John the Baptist, or St. Paul.

The *inspired* man of the reformation, after he had been dogmatizing for some time, received a gentle chiding for his boldness and temerity from Pope Leo X. Luther replied: "Most Blessed Father, the propositions which I set forth, are in the form of *theses*, or *inquiries*, they are not put forth as *doctrines*. Now, what can I do? I am surrounded on all sides by learned men of great brilliancy of talents, and of profound eloquence. I am obliged to speak out among them, like a goose screeching in the company of swans. If I cannot retract, I will explain. Most Blessed Father, give me life, or give me death; approve or disapprove; I will hear your voice as the voice of Jesus Christ." *Epistle to Leo* X, Trinity Sunday, 1518, a long time after Luther had become *inspired* (?)

To Thomas de Vio, Cardinal Cajetan, Legate of the Pope, the *inspired* man wrote, several months after his epistle to the Pope:—"My only desire is to hear the voice of the Church and to follow it." *Epistle to Cajetan, Festival of St. Luke, Evangelist,* 1518. Pretty fair specimen of submission to the authority of the Church and of the Pope, on the part of an individual who subscribed himself:—"Martin Luther, by the Grace of God Evangelist of Wittemberg, by the revelation of Jesus Christ." *Luther's Works, Epistles, tome* ii.

April 20, 1529, at Spires, a noted city of Germany, the "Imperial Diet" was in session. Six princes of the Empire and the deputies of fourteen free cities presented to the "Diet," in writing, a "Protest" against a certain edict which commanded that the peace of the Empire should no further be endangered by prolonged toleration of seditious disturbers of the true faith,—whose objects, at bottom, were political, not religious. The Pro-testants appealed to a General Council. "Young idea" was now in its twelfth year, without a special name. Thenceforth the thing was called Protestantism. This was five years after Luther wrote himself:—"An Evangelist by the Grace of God, not from man, but by the revelation of Jesus Christ," *tome* ii, as above quoted.

June 13, 1525, old style, the trumpets of Cupid, all of a sudden, and to the astonishment of the Empire, sounded forth an *Epithalamium* around the so-called marital couch of the new Evangelist. The inspired man himself tells how it was, and gives the *legal* genealogical results. "On June 13, 1525, I married; on June 6, 1526, my first child *John* was born; in 1527, my second child Elizabeth;" and he goes on recounting the successive appearance, in due intervals, of Magdalene, Martin, Paul, and lastly, in 1534, Margaret. Plentiful as evidences of this continent's re-discovery by the Spaniards in 1492, are the evidences, from Luther's own writings, from the pens of contemporary authors, and from the writings and collections of Luther's works, published by his own disciples, concerning that marriage and its corollaries. The event, and what followed, became "common gossip" in Germany. See English translation of Audin's *Life of Luther*, for references to original documentary proofs ; it would be a needless task for us to transcribe the scores of said easily accessible references. The marriage was a hurried affair; Justus Jonas, Lucas Cranach and wife, and Dr. Pomer, were the only witnesses. Kate Bora, in fact, made it known in plain Dutch to Martin, that she would "put up with no more of his nonsense unless they got married at once," and so the thing had to be done! Not long after the marriage ceremony something happened about which Erasmus, contemporary writers, and even Martin Luther himself, were by no means reticent. Martin and Kate were married, as the ceremony was called, June 13, 1525. On the subsequent fourteenth day, June 27, 1525, the newly married poor woman became terribly afflicted with a painful complaint which medical diagnosis specificated as premonitory symptoms of *dolor parturientis*, but on the fifteenth day the suffering patient was pronounced to be 'getting along as well as could be expected." It proved to be a boy, weight about ten pounds avoirdupois. On the fifteenth day after the nuptials, eleven months and ten days afterward, June 6, 1526, JOHN, the first born, according to law, came in on time. In the interim of waiting for JOHN, as we have it narrated by John Aurifaber, beloved disciple and boon friend of the newly-married Evangelist, *Tisch-Reden*, part ii, page 20, edit. Francfort, 1569, Martin Luther gave utterance to feelings of pity and condolence for his poor dear "*uxor gravida*" in these plaintive words :- -" *Es ist schwer zwei Gæste*

zu ernæhren, den einen im Haus, den andern vor der Thur.
Some years subsequently, to Jerome Weller, Martin
wrote a letter and described how severely he was obliged
to "use the rod upon my son Andrew to get any good of
him." *Coll. Lat. Opera Luth.*, tome ii, p. 226. From all
accounts sent down to posterity by his daddy, "my son
Andrew" must have been what the pulpit actor at the
Plymouth, Brooklyn, would call "a pretty hard cuss."
They seem to have had a terrible time, poor Martin and
Kate, curbing the pranks of that fifteen-day scamp—that
merry "Andrew" of the incipient *Reformation!* O that
rod and "my son Andrew!" what a tale they do unfold!
So-called marriages became, forthwith, the order of the
day among renegade sacrilegious vow-breakers, whose
prompting passions easily induced them to follow their
inspired leader's *reforming* example, to the great scandal
of Christendom, to the very increase of shameful immor-
alities, and to the wonderful and rapid multiplication of
merry "Andrews." We refer to this state of affairs because it has an important bearing upon a fact of history
which we intend to impress upon the reader's mind before concluding this chapter.

A. D. 1530, Protestantism was in its thirteenth year,
ten years after its solemn condemnation by a decree of
Pope Leo X. The Protestant princes, the ecclesiastical
chiefs of the Reformation who were of the German Empire, and the deputies of fourteen free cities, appointed
Martin Luther, Justus Jonas, Philip Melancthon, and
the famed Pomeranus, to draw up a precise and full
"Confession of Faith," that all the world might know
the exact foundation upon which Protestantism was to
find a base upon which it could rest. The work was
completed with great care. It was sent to the princes
and deputies; by them it was referred back to Luther

alone; it was finally polished, as to language and style, by Philip Melancthon, the man of *belles lettres* among the reformers. Luther, before the final return of the document to the princes for presentation to the world, gave the last touch with his own hand, and wrote this remarkable endorsement:---" Whoever teaches the contrary to this confession of faith, let him be condemned."

June 25, 1530, in presence of the Emperor, and of all the actual members of the "Diet," the confession of Faith called the " Augsburg Confession " was read. To provide against further attemps at innovation the Emperor caused the princes and all others concerned to be asked whether they dissented in any other particulars from the doctrines of the Catholic Church, or had other abuses to complain of. After mature deliberation they answered that .the document there present "contained all they dissented from." The princes and all the others who were of the Empire affixed their signatures to that " Confession of Augsburg." We have noticed, particularly, Martin Luther's endorsement. See *Pallav.*, book iii, chap. 3; *Waterworth's* " Council of Trent," and "Original Histories " in general. One must destroy all the great libraries of Germany and the archives of the "Imperial Diet," as well as the " State Papers " of the various petty courts of the Empire, before one particle of what we set forth in this pamphlet, regarding the treated question, can be successfully invalidated or questioned. Of course, such reading matter is not to be found in our Public School Libraries, or other reading books. That would never do!

Those of Zurich, Strasburg, and other places, desired to sign and adopt the "Confession of Augsburg," but they wanted the omission of the sixth article, which admitted the " Real Presence." Upon that point, and upon no other, there was, then, a separating difference of opinion among the reformers.

So, good reader, "Analytical Treatment of History" makes it plainly evident to all the world, that at Augsburg, June 25, 1530, except as to doctrine about the Holy Eucharist----CHANG leaning one way and ENG the other----universal Protestantism, in the thirteenth year of its age, stood up in the presence of the whole world and swore to its "Confession of Faith." The Confession contained twenty-one articles and seven objected abuses. At the close of the articles the Protestants declare before God that in the whole of their faith "there is nothing at variance with the Scriptures, with the Catholic, or even with the Roman Church, in so far as that doctrine is known to them from the writers of that Church." Moreover, the said Protestants complain most bitterly that they are stigmatized as heretics, whereas, their faith is that of the Roman Church; and the disagreement is only about some few abuses which had crept into the Church without any clear or certain authority in their favor." Besides all this, the "Confession" distinctly acknowledges the obligation of all men to receive and obey the first six General Councils. *Augsburg Confess.*, and authors, *passim.* Verily, it seems that the temporal and spiritual originating heads of the reformation did not feel very sensitively any inspiring influence from heaven bidding them go out from Rome!

It is a well know fact of history that Martin Luther did, in writing, pledge himself most solemnly to the Pope's legate, that he would maintain silence for the future, if his opponents would do the same, and, if they would "allow the thing to *die out* of itself." Moreover, he would "acknowledge the excessive severity of his language toward his opponents," and he would "publish a writing wherein he would exhort the people to adhere to the pure worship of the Church of Rome;" finally, he would "write such a letter to the Roman Pontiff as would prove his desire of reconciliation. Luther did write that letter. Read this quotation:—"And now, most beloved Father, I protest before God and all His creatures, that I have never intended to touch or prejudice, by any craft, the power of the Roman Church, or, of Your Blessedness. Yea, I must fully confess that the power of that Church is above all things; and that nothing in earth or heaven ought to be ranked above it." *Luther's Epistle*. Mark that language from a man who had been, for years, laboring under inspiration from somewhere, to pull down the Pope and the Church concerning which he pens the above sentiments. "Catholic" and "Average" often get at it about the inspiration of Luther. No difference of opinion exists as to the fact of the inspiration! the dispute is always about the appropriate appellation of the inspiring prompter.

It is a well known fact of history that, in Germany, all the chiefs, temporal and spiritual, of Protestantism wanted, A. D. 1530, to get back into the fold of the Holy Catholic Church, but failing to gain readmittance, they therefore, in spite of themselves, remained outside the pale of the One Church, and became the first sources of the innumerable "sects," which at this day call themselves by the anti-Christian name Protestant--protesting against the positive teachings of Christ's only Church. Why all this? Why did not the return take place? The writer will essay an explanation.

Philip Melancthon was the head man of polite literature among the reformers. He was the favorite of Luther, a sort of "official secretary" and "chief of staff" to young Protestantism on all state and ceremonial occasions. We will make official use of Philip for a short time. We have noticed Luther's anxiety, real or pretended, to return to the Church, with sincere obedience to the Holy Father in all things. On certain conditions Martin would let the thing "die out of itself." We must place the "official secretary" upon the witness stand, to disclose further about the status of this affair, in which all Protestantism of the day was deeply interested. To thinking men it must be of surpassing interest, even at this late period of the catastrophe. Well, princes and ecclesiastical chiefs are desirous of reconciliation with the Church! The Cenfession of Augsburg was, again, carefully scrutinized. Philip Melancthon was deputized by the Protestant princes to make proposals to the Papal legate that, if a reconciliation could be effected on the basis they proposed, they were willing and anxious to return to the Church. The petition was a unanimous one, and thus say the petitioners :—"The authority of the Roman Pontiff is, by us, respectfully reverenced, as well as is, also, the whole ecclesiastical polity."

Melancthon made a report to the Emperor in these words :—"The Lutheran question is not so complicated and unseemly as Your Majesty fancies. The whole controversy is reducible to three points. The two kinds in the Sacrament of the Lord's Supper, the abolition of private masses, and *the marriage of the pastors.* If we could agree upon these articles it would be easy to come to an understanding upon the others."

A carefully prepared proposition was drawn up, and in the name of all the German reformers, ecclesiastics and princes, was officially presented to the Papal legate, September 1530. The Protestant party of the Empire was a unit in submitting the proposition as a final settlement. Calvin or Henry VIII had not been, as yet, much afflicted with the prevailing inspirations of the day, and the Sacramentarians of Switzerland were not on good terms with Luther's friends concerning the question of the "real presence." Here, therefore, we speak of Protestantism as existing September 1530--the only recognizable, in some way organized, Protestantism of which, at that time, the world had a knowledge. The carefully prepared proposition which Protestantism submitted to the Papal legate was worded in this form :—

"If a few things were conceded, or dissembled, concord might be restored, to wit:—if both kinds were allowed to ours, and the marriage of priests and monks were tolerated. If it should not seem expedient for these things to be openly granted, they might still be dissembled under some kind of pretext, as for example, that these things may drag on till the assembling of a Council. As regards the mass, also, some method may be found by good and learned men to prevent that from being any longer a source of division; we, on our part, will agree to restore obedience to the Bishops."

It is needless to enter into further details about negotiations which were carried on for some time. There followed no beneficial practical results. We are treating the subject from no other stand-point than that of undeniable history, and our statements and quotations are unanswerable. Our facts of history are most clear and positive proofs to the world of intellect, regarding the true "why and wherefore" of the continued "dragging along" of Protestantism, and of the relentless hatred of Roman Supremacy displayed by Protestants--after the Church of Rome, faithful, still faithful to St. Paul's injunctions, *Rom.* xvi, 17, had *marked* them, and had put them, their novelties and abuses, outside the pale of Christ's One Fold. "Essays on the Internal and External History of the Council of Trent," prefixed to Waterworth's translation of "The Canons and Decrees of the Council of Trent," published by the Dunigans, New York, 1848, gives the original texts of our quotations, with references to books and pages of the works of the reformers, published by themselves. Melancthon's letters to the Pope's legate are dated August 5, and August 22, 1530, letter to Luther, September 1, same year, and the FINAL PROPOSAL of the whole body, for reconciliation, bears date September 22, 1530. We have already remarked, and remark anew, that the archives of the petty courts of Germany, and of the old Empire, must be put out of existence, even if the writings of the reformers themselves were not in evidence, before our demonstration of the *situation*, A. D. 1530, from "Analytical Treatment of History," can have the shadow of a doubt reflected upon it.

Here is a summary of the situation:-- The chiefs of Protestantism, all, ecclesiastics and princes, agreed with Luther, that the voice of the Bishop of Rome was to be regarded as the voice of Jesus Christ Himself! (Papal Infallibility most intense!) They would all return to the bosom of the Catholic Church, if the Catholic Church would receive them! The princes would forego further plundering of Church property, and would arrange, in some satisfactory way, about already-perpetrated robberies. The receiving of the Sacrament under one kind need not be insisted on. The little change in the manner of celebrating mass would not be urged. All charges of *novelties* and *abuses*, so recklessly and lyingly made against the Catholic Church, were *nollied*, as the lawyers say. What, then, in the name of truth, prevented the union from becoming an accomplished fact? History furnishes but one answer. All obstacles to re-union

19

were readily adjustable, save one. The bread-craving merry "Andrews" of the reformation, and their unappeasable mammas, constituted the one sole grand obstacle upon which Protestantism grounded--and upon which it remained aground. The married ecclesiastics among the chiefs would have the Catholic Church to "connive," to "dissemble," to let Protestant novelties and abuses "drag on" until they would "die out of themselves." But the Catholic Church had not received from Jesus Christ to "dissemble" or to "compromise" in matters of Faith and Morals, and the door o Catholicity was shut in the faces---not of the individuals if they would repent and amend---but of their outrageous novelties and abuses. They clung to the poor fellows in spite of diplomacy, kept them out, and made them set up house keeping for themselves. All their subsequent and present outcries against " Papal pretensions and innovations " furnish to every clear headed historical searcher for truth a splendid exemplification of Roman Supremacy and Papal Infallibility---for the Pope alone was competent to pronounce, and did pronounce in their case.

This "Old Catholic" thinks that he has set forth in a few very intelligible paragraphs a complete, and an explanatory history of the secession movement which men call the Protestant Reformation. During the progress of negotiations for re-admission to the Catholic Church, Staupitz, Miltisch, Crotus, and a great number of others, acknowledged their errors and became reconciled, to the great joy of the Church, but we search in vain for an instance of a married priest or monk who returned. Repentance never once sat by the pillow of any one of them, even when dying. See *Audin*, vol. 2, d. 215. As to that class of his followers Luther had made no miscalculation. Inspired as he was from below, the heresiarch well knew that every marriage of a priest bound to his cause a lost being who would beget others of his own stamp, and thus we can readily understand the warfare against celibacy which he commenced at Wartzburg and continued through life.

Candid American non-Catholic reader, we, as you may notice, narrate plain facts, and to the point, in plain words and from accessible first sources. The *American* mind, which is not a *Protestant* mind, far from it, is susceptible to, and impressible by FACTS, when it çan have the facts and can *realize* the plain inducing motives and causes of said facts. No Catholic divine or educated Catholic layman ever hesitates to face the plainest facts of history, in so far as said facts have a bearing upon the One Church of Jesus Christ. In the field of history anti-Catholics *make* quaker guns and point them at Catholicity. When *we* choose to dislodge the dressed-up and painted make-believes, and think it worth while to advance upon the positions of the Munchausen gunners, every experienced ear recognizes at once the ring of our true metal. The writer has just asserted that the *American* mind is not a *Protestant* mind. Throughout this little book he has ventured upon no assertion without being prepared to support the same with positive proofs from first sources. He, therefore, as to the last assertion also, will satisfy the *American* mind with proof positive. This a Protestant country, indeed! It is not a Catholic country, we grant--it is not a Protestant country, we prove. A population may not all be Cotholic-- it must be a rascally logic that would, therefore, set down the NONS as being, all of them, actual Protestants! The revised census, as the official figures of the Bureau of Statistics exhibits, 1871, gives the total population of the United States, 38.555.983, including whites, blacks, reds, and yellows. Carefully prepared statistics, published 1867, *Cincinnati Commercial*, August 9, 1871, show that, in the United States, there were 30.347.088 persons who were *not* Protestants--who disclaimed connection with any Protestant organization. Now, 38.555.983, less 30.347.088, demonstrate a result of 8.208.895 Protestants in the United States. We will be generous and give them credit for the round number, at present, of eight and a quarter millions, divided into innumerable little Protestant sects--sects numerous, but none of them strong, their only bond of union being a common battle-cry of *protest* against the Old Church--a protest which proclaims that when Jesus Christ declared that He would be with His Church forever, teaching all truth, and when He promised that the gates of hell should never prevail against that Church, the Redeemer did not mean what He said, or was not God enough to keep his declared promise. That is Protestantism! That is what the *protest* means! And this is a Protestant country, forsooth!

The separate pieces of Protestantism form an aggregate of eight and a quarter millions of individuals'; but there are thirty and a quarter millions of individuals in the country who are not Protestants; therefore this is a Protestant country! Shades of Aristotle, how that syllogism limps! And, O dear, this is a Protestant country! Among the thirty and a quarter millions who are *not* Protestants, how many, thinkest thou, are Catholics--including good practical Catholics and the non-practical, to whose minds there is no greater torture in life than the fear of "dying without the priest?" How many? Dr. Dœllinger, in our next section, suggests the question.

Will the *New York Freeman's Journal*, or some other competent truth-searcher, make and publish a reliable statement for the edification of all concerned? We have no access to data of *authenticated* figures, but we would like to be "posted." He shall have our thanks and deserve a magnificent premium who, first, shall exhibit a fair showing of the numerical difference, in the United States, between the professors of spiritual allegiance to the One Faith of the Holy Catholic Church and the professors of any kind of adhesion to the *aggregate* one thousand and one noisy little sects. And, O dear, if the twenty-two or twenty-three millions of our fellow Americans who are neither Catholics nor Protestants will only condescend to reason the case by the nonsensical lights of Protestant logic and Protestant mathematics, perhaps their decision may be that this is now, or soon will be, a Catholic country. And, O dear, wouldn't that be a frightful state of affairs? Wouldn't the Republic then be in danger? Only just think of it! EIGHT millions of Catholics, and only THIRTY millions to keep them in check! O dear, and alas, this Protestant country!

In the year 1856 this writer heard from the lips of Ex-Governor Mathews, of Mississippi, an account of a terrible consternation produced by *know-nothing* preachers of that day in a certain locality of his State. Horrors of Popery and a dreaded uprising of Papists were the favorite themes. The Governor spoke of Native Americans who used never go to bed at night without an axe ready at the head of the bed for fear of the foreign Papists, whilst the census of population gave the numerical strength of the Papists in that locality and the five contiguous counties, one old man and his wife, and three Negroes, all native American Catholics from Maryland. If they had taken a notion to rise what *would* have become of the brave inhabitants of those six counties of chivalrous Mississippi!

XXXIV.

CRUMBS OF COMFORT FOR ANTI-CATHOLIC PROPHETS.

The unfoldings of this section of CATENA AUREA will enable every clear-minded reader to comprehend the exact pretendings of *Dœllingerism;* will enable every such reader to discuss the situation intelligently. Would that we were compelled to "stop the press" to announce that the latest hope of anti-Catholics had developed himself into a Lacordaire, but the time is not yet. The "movement" has not yet accomplished all the good for the true Catholic cause which a permitting Providence designs that it shall produce. In the religious world Dœllinger fostering "a new departure," and Bismarck "warring against Papal Supremacy," are only a couple of bogus shillings nailed to the counter of Christianity that all lovers of honesty may compare them with the lawful coin, and thus become good judges of the "queer," eventually to despise the baseness of the bogus issue and the witless folly of the base issuers.

We take the liberty of reproducing from the *Cincinnati Commercial's* Supplement of August 9, 1871, p. 2, col. 3, and from the *New York Freeman's Journal* of August 26, 1871, p. 4, col. 5, the outspoken opinion of Dr. Dœllinger himself on the situation; and, also, the plain words of Pope Pius IX respecting the practical meaning of Papal Infallibility. We give these truthful reports from known and reliable European sources, so that no reader need hesitate to give the proper title to all the "stuff and nonsense" which *telegrams* and *own specials* retail concerning that vast little movement against the Catholic Church in a corner of Germany.

A wide awake and "well posted" American gentleman had a long conversation with Dr. Dœllinger at Munich, a synopsis of which was transmitted to the *New York World* under date July 22, 1871. In course of conversation the Doctor said:

"Tell the Americans that I am a Catholic still, and hope to die a Catholic; and that nothing would grieve me more than to be the cause of schism in the Church."

Dr. Dœllinger questioned his visitor at some length concerning Catholicity in the United States. The gentleman had with him, and exhibited some statistics concerning the numerical strength of the Protestant and Catholic Churches in the United States. The Doctor seemed delighted by the confirmation of statements on the same subject which he had received from other sources. Said he:

"It appears by these figures that there were in the United States, in 1867, an aggregate of 30.347.088 persons who were not Protestants; how many of these were Catholics? The little Protestant sects seem to be very numerous, but none of them appears to be strong."

The gentleman remarked that there was a very general belief that these "little Protestant sects" were about to be increased by one more, at the head of which would be Dr. Dœllinger.

"No," said he, with earnestness; "believe me, it is not so. They call me 'the new Luther.' Heaven forbid! I have no ambition to play the part of Luther, there is no Catherine Bora who is luring me away. I am excommunicated, it is true; but I am not a schismatic. And, pray, clearly understand that I have, and can have, no sympathy whatever with the errors of Protestantism. I have spent most of my life in combatting these errors, and I am annoyed now to find that Protestant clergymen and theologians imagine that I am in sympathy with them, or have changed my opinions. Do they forget my 'Doc-

trine de l'Eucharistie dans les Trois Premiers Siecles,' my work ' On the
Interior Development and the Effects of the Lutheran Schism,' and my
' Sketch of Luther?' Ah, sir, I see clearly enough that the sudden notoriety which has been given to my humble name arises, not from
sympathy with my desire to preserve the Holy Catholic Church from
what I think is an error, but from hatred to her, and a desire to bring
about her destruction. Vain desire! for she is built upon a rock, and
the gates of hell shall not prevail against her!"

The interviewer spoke, but guardedly, of the difficulty
of logic which presented itself to men who, like the Doctor, declared that the Church was infallible and its infallible utterances were delivered by the voice of a General Council, but who also affirmed that, in the case of
the dogma pronounced on the 18th of last July, this infallible voice had uttered a falsehood. " Dr. Dœllinger,"
writes the gentleman, "skillfully put aside this point,
and by a transition very adroitly made. He went on to
tell that some informal negotiations had been going on
between himself and the authorities at Rome, with the
object of bringing about a reconciliation." " From the
manner rather than the words of Dr. Dœllinger," continues the American writer, " I inferred--perhaps wrong-
fully--that he did not deem such a reconciliation impossible, although, as he himself said, in all such concilia-
tions it is not Rome that yields anything."

The interviewer says that when he came to speak of
the dogma against which his interlocutor had revolted,
it was easy to see how very deeply the Doctor's feelings
were enlisted, and how he had imparted into this question of theology political ideas. When questioned as to
whether Papal Infallibility was not understood to be
restricted to spiritual matters only, Dr. Dœllinger again
made rather an evasive reply, saying that under the
interpretation of the dogma which would likely be given
by the Roman Curia, it would be difficult to draw the

line between spiritual and worldly matters. "**As yet,**" said the Doctor, with a smile, "as yet, the movement has not progressed far. Out of eight thousand priests in Bavaria there are NOT ONE HUNDRED with me."

Our American writer asked Dr. Dœllinger if there was any organized party of which he was the head, or whether the opponents of Infallibility were acting without concert with each other.

" There," replied he, " you touch upon a very important point, and one which I should be glad to have well understood. When I speak, I express only my own sentiments. But it is evident that there is a large body of people who adhere to this movement who have nothing in common with me. I constantly receive letters and addresses signed by Atheists, by Israelites, and by Protestants, and to all of these it is evident that the interior character of the movement which I have set on foot has not the slightest interest. They wish to attack and over-throw the Catholic religion ; I, devoted to that religion, seek only to save it from what seems to be an error. Nevertheless, throughout all the world there is a hatred of ultramontanism and a recognition of the necessity of erecting a barrier against the doctrines of the personal infallibility of the Pope. If all who share this sentiment were actu-ated by my opinions, I could welcome them as allies ; but, as the great majority of them are inspired by nothing better than a hatred of all Christianity, I can have no association with them. It is certainly to be feared that the reform inside the Church will be forgotten and overwhelmed in the attack made upon the Church from without. I confess that one who takes issue with the Church, animated by the best of motives, treads on dangerous ground. In my case, I plant myself upon the position that I am not in conflict with the true mind of the Church and that the Council did not express truly, in the dogma of the 18th of July, the mind of the Church. The truth is in the bosom of the Church ; we must believe that, or we go adrift at once. I say to you that it is certain that when dissidents pass beyound limits that are perhaps not well known, they fall into the abyss, into nihil-ism. We have seen too many proofs of this. And I confess that while, in all of the addresses I receive, I easily find the negation, the denial of the dogma of infallibility, I look in vain, among elements so diverse, for an affirmative agreement. But all that we desire are tentative measures; provisional measures for repelling the dogma, and for maintaining the just rights of the civil power, which this dogma, in our opinion, invades.

The chatty American says that the interview saddened him. The interesting communication is brought to a close in this wise :--

"It left on my mind the impression that Dr. Dœllinger was himself convinced that the movement he had set on foot would be soon swallowed up in the advancing wave of rationalism and skepticism. As for Dr. Dœllinger himself, I should not be at all surprised to hear at any moment that he had made his submission. He is clearly ill at ease, and he is too much of a logician to fail to see that his present position is untenable. He must advance or retreat. If he were a Luther, he would advance. But he derides Luther, and I fancy he is more like Lacordaire."

And so, after all, the parturient throes of the Bavarian mountain can give birth to nothing but a ridiculous mouse! The great analyzer of history only fears that, "under the interpretation of the dogma which would likely be given by the Roman Curia, it would be difficult to draw the line between spiritual and worldly matters!" And the Doctor and his friends, not *ignorantly*, but mendaciously and *Cæsarly*, would school people into false notions about the definition of the Vatican Council. They would "make believe" that the said definition implies a declaration of a divine right, inherent in the Papal office, to interfere with the political affairs of secular governments. The highest authority on earth, with holy indignation, but with meekest firmness of words, flings the satanic insinuation in the teeth of the false knaves. The following words are to the point:

WHAT PIO NONO DECLARES.

On a late occasion, receiving a deputation of the "Roman Academy for the Advancement of the Catholic

Religion," made up of Catholic men of learning, the Holy Father said :

"Among the many questions that are mooted, there is one that especially should be refuted. It is the false idea that the enemy strives to give of Pontifical Infallibility. The enemy tries to include, under this Infallibility, the right of deposing Sovereigns, and releasing their subjects from their obligations of fidelity.

" It is true, such a right was once exercised, by many Popes, in many countries, in extreme cases. But that had no relation whatever to the doctrine of Papal Infallibility. It was not as Infallible, but as *Pope*, that some of my Predecessors exercised this power. It was not as of the essence of their office, but grew out of the political order of the ancient society of Europe.

" The States of Europe were constituted as Catholics. They chose to see in their Pope not only his ecclesiastical Sovereignty, that he holds from God, but to attribute to him, also, a civil and a political prerogative, that he had only from the free choice of nations, some of which chose him as supreme Civil Judge, even to the right of deposing kings and princes.

" At the present time, the condition of things is widely different. Nothing but intended bad faith could confound the dogmatical infallibility, given by a special grace to the Successor of St. Peter, in regard to matters that are of the revealed deposit of the Faith, with a human arrangement, undertaken by some of the Popes, for the public good, at the importunity of the peoples interested.

" No honest man dreams of the resumption of such powers, at this day. The Sovereign Pontiff thinks of such a step less than any one. These are mere pretexts, to excite the minds of some princes against the Church."

THE AUTHOR'S OWN COROLLARY.

One of these days William of Berlin, who styles himself "Emperor of Germany, by the grace of God," is going to DICTATE to the United States of America, and to Great Britain, the terms upon which they *must* settle the "Alabama claims," and, also, that foreign Emperor will decree, finally, whether we or our former stepmother shall have the sovereignty of a certain island of the ocean, about the title to which there has been much disputing. We all shall be perfectly satisfied with the dictation and with the decree, and shall abide by the terms and decision, because, virtually, they will be our own acts by our own chosen umpire. But then, dear and candid American reader, had not the "Joint Highs" of the middle ages as much right to choose and constitute an umpire and final judge of their international and home complications as modern "Joint Highs" had and exercised in the instance under notice? Had not the freemen of those days as much right to choose their common Father, the Pope, as that umpire, as we had to choose Kaiser Wilhelm of the Hohenzollerns?

If U. S. and G. B. had sufficient greatness and enough independence of intellect to allow them to request the Pope to take testimony and give judgment with regard to their international entanglements, as free governments used to do "in days of auld lang syne," most assuredly they would have the *Alabama* and the *San Juan* misunderstandings passed upon and adjusted according to the true meaning of the sacerdotal URIM and THUMMIM, and His Holiness himself, and every other Catholic, now as then, would smile at the innocent verdancy, or the verdant ignorance, of any one who would predicate of the Papacy in such matters either "highest perfection of the knowing faculty," or infallibility of human judgment.

☞ Respected reader, "An Old Catholic" would like to say yet many things touching upon Papal spiritual authority, and something, too, about the temporal relations—but space is limited and, for the present, he forbears. Before we part, however, please take mental notice that the prime sources of our TELEGRAMS and SPECIALS are ITALIAN JOURNALS. Just now, and for a purpose, the leading Journals of Italy are owned and controlled by Jews. The fact has gone the rounds of the American press, but, of course, without comment. Infidels join hands with the Jews, for the nonce, because both would extirpate Christianity if it could be done. The bigoted among Protestants applaud the doings of the infidels and Jews because of their own unpleasant feelings toward the Papacy—but, for all that, the Pope is the Vicar of Christ, and CHRIST IS GOD. God is not to be mocked, nor is the Holy Catholic Church pressed for time! "Adhuc modicum et videbimus magnalia Dei!"

CHAPTER TWELFTH.

XXXV.

HOW TO SEEK AND FIND CATHOLIC TRUTH.

It has been the misfortune of modern non-Catholics of America to be born to the inheritance of "protesting." The Catholic Church does not look upon them, individually, as formal heretics. They only become so by willful obstinacy in resisting the grace of God. By God's goodness many and many favorable opportunities are thrown in their way, whereby they may come to a knowledge of true faith, and thus save their own souls. What will it avail a man if he gain the whole world and lose his own soul? *St. Matth.* xv. 26. In the end it will prove a frightful bargain. As it is, our modern non-Catholic friends, many of them possessed of noblest minds and most unprejudiced feelings, are oppressed with false ideas about Catholic faith and Catholic practices. They are thus oppressed because the said ideas have been school-booked, and dictionaried, and public-lectured, into their intellects, in spite of themselves, by force of circumstances over which they had no control. But in this country the pressure does not continue beyond a few of the earliest years of life, and the oppressed thus become at liberty to examine the evidences upon which they have been induced to think thus and so about the matter of religion. To the sincere man searching for a knowledge of what he must do to save his soul, the sufficient grace of God will never be wanting. Divine grace will guide human reason until that reason finds a solid foundation upon which it may base the true faith which will please God and conduct the believer to heaven. This "Old Catholic" recommends to every well-meaning searcher for God's truth our Catholic plan, so plainly set forth, page 37 of this pamphlet. Moreover, dear searcher, the same "Old Catholic" begs you, for God's sake and your soul's, to ponder, and reason from, "Our First Principle," page 39. That first principle is as self-evidently true as any first principle of Philosophy or principle of the exact sciences. A course of reasoning from that self-evident first principle will lead every correct reasoner, straight-forward, into the pale of the Holy Catholic Church, and, of a consequence, to a necessary recognition of the abso-lute truth of that old-time, primitive, article of faith which we call Papal Infallibility.

Almost every Catholic priest, at his own home, can furnish to every sincere inquirer for truth a full exhibit of evidences *demonstrating* the Holy Catholic Church to be the true and only Church of Jesus Christ. The lips of our priests keep knowledge, and, by God's grace, they are prepared and know how to impart the same. Go, dear non-Catholic reader, go with confidence to the near-est Catholic priest and ask for knowledge. Go with con-fidence, sure of a fatherly reception and most considerate treatment. If you need the excuse of an introduction, take this little BROCHURE in your hand, and IT will intro-duce you. Our word for it, the first visit will not be the last. Go, show yourself to the priest. *St. Luke* v, 14. It is not a matter of great difficulty, now-a-days, for men of good will to find that greatest of all blessings on earth--Catholic truth--and thus to save their souls.

XXXVI.
A CONCLUDING ILLUSTRATION.

In the course of his past reading, this "Old Catholic," he forgets where, met with what he considers to be an apt illustration of the proper method for one to pursue in order to learn and appreciate the real tenets which the Catholic Church holds and teaches. The writer begs as a favor that each non-Catholic reader will give to the illustration the mental pondering of a passing moment:--

"There is, indeed, a vast difference between the Catholic Church and her doctrines, as they appear to those outside her pale and to those who have been admitted within it. There is a wonderful difference between the appearance of a beautiful painted cathedral window, as seen from the outside and as seen from within the sacred edifice which it adorns. To an external observer there is presented nothing distinct and clear to attract attention and admiration of hidden beauties; all seems to be a confused mass of intermingled daubs of dingy and varied colors, dismal to the eye of the beholder, and inviting, as it were, the careless gazer to pass on.

"Within the edifice the confused mass disappears into beautiful designs; the dingy hue clears up into colors of surpassing brilliancy and most precious composition of magnificent outlines, which are reflected in rainbow tints on surrounding objects. Even from without, to him who was not an utterly careless gazer, there was a certain shadowing forth, a dim augury of the glories within. But to those alone who have passed the threshold, does the work reveal its splendid wonders, or disclose its glorious significance."

How apt the illustration! A convert to Catholicity, much better than one who is "to the manor born," can feel the force of the illustration. Outside the pale of the Catholic Church her beauties and her glories may not attract attention; but, within, there are other magnificent visions of her splendid and harmonious parts. The strength of her divine organization, the grand unity of all her doctrines, the plain and open pathway to heaven, are seen and appreciated. The glorious Church foretold and described by the prophets of old--that Church, which, in fullness of time was founded by Jesus Christ upon the " Rock "--that Church stands revealed. Within, indeed, the shining sun-light of heaven makes the evidences stand out in bold relief. O, Glorious Holy Catholic Church! Thou only city of God upon earth! "O, Mother! whoever is a child of God is also thy child; after the lapse of so many ages, thou art yet fruitful." "O Church of Rome, whence Peter will forever strengthen his brethren, let my right hand forget itself if I ever forget thee! Let my tongue cleave to my mouth and be motionless, if thou be not to the last breath of my life the principal object of my joy and of my rejoicings!" The last exclamations are thine, great and good Archbishop Fenelon of Cambray. Permit " An Old Catholic " of America to borrow thy eminently Catholic words, and from his inmost soul most earnestly to repeat them, as if his own.

Christian outsider, dost thou seek and desire to know, with infallible certainty, where Christ dwelleth? The Holy Catholic Church, in the name and by the authority of Jesus Christ Himself, most lovingly inviteth thee to "COME AND SEE!" *St. John* i, 39.

FINIS.